"I am in need of a wife who is all woman!"

Cherry quivered in panic from the heat of Lucien's breath against her cheek, from eyes smoldering a message of purpose, of anticipated pleasure, of intimacy.

Torrid seconds later she had been rendered blind to reason by an expert seducer whose kisses and caresses had transported her to a limbo of bliss.

"Tonight, *ma chérie,* when I introduce you to Riviera society, you will no longer be able to fool them into thinking that your lovely, ice-cool body has never melted in the heat of a man's desire!"

Her sensation of floating on a passion-dark cloud intensified when he swept her off her feet, using his mouth to silence her weak moan of protest....

Books by Margaret Rome

Harlequin Romances

Harlequin Presents

These books may be available at your local bookseller.

For a free catalog listing all titles currently available,
send your name and address to:

Harlequin Reader Service
2504 West Southern Avenue, Tempe, AZ 85282
Canadian address: Stratford, Ontario N5A 6W2

Bay of Angels

Margaret Rome

Harlequin Books

TORONTO • NEW YORK • LONDON
AMSTERDAM • PARIS • SYDNEY • HAMBURG
STOCKHOLM • ATHENS • TOKYO • MILAN

Original hardcover edition published in 1983
by Mills & Boon Limited

ISBN 0-373-02584-X

Harlequin Romance first edition November 1983

Printed in U.S.A.

CHAPTER ONE

'Isn't this simply *too* much!' Diana Dermot breathed blissfully across the shoulder of her friend as they stood on the balcony of their hotel bedroom contemplating a moonlit harbour crammed with yachts flying flags of all nations, and a brilliantly illuminated boulevard draped like a scintillating necklace between the curving shoulders of the most famous, fabulous, exorbitantly expensive strip of coast in the whole of Europe, a place where every few seconds sumptuous limousines purred to a halt outside hotels designed and furbished to resemble miniature palaces.

'Even now,' Diana continued, 'after three days and nights spent soaking in this fantastic atmosphere, I still can't believe my luck! Pinch me, Cherry,' she urged, 'convince me that we're actually in Cannes, staying in a top-class hotel during Film Festival week, and all for a mere pittance!'

In spite of an inner despondency Cherry managed to muster a smile.

'I don't know why you're finding it so difficult to believe you've achieved your ambition,' she teased mildly. 'You're such a determined baggage, Diana. Usually you decide what you want and then chart a course straight towards it, but this time you used a more devious route towards your objective. I must be as naïve as you maintain, because it's only during the past few days that I've begun to realise why you decided to forsake your career in the theatre in favour of a nine-to-five job in a travel agency. In fact,' she scolded as gently as she was able, 'I'm beginning to suspect that the circumstances that gave rise to our arrival in Cannes were not based on good fortune as you implied, but were cleverly contrived!'

Seemingly quite unabashed by the note of censure in her friend's voice, Diana grinned.

'Acting is my life, as you know very well, Cherry, I could never absent myself from the theatre permanently. I took a job at the agency purely as a temporary measure, following a hunch that's paid off beautifully! One of the perks attached to working for a travel firm is being offered last-minute cancellations at rock bottom prices, but not even I, devious and determined though I may be, am capable of manipulating the wife of a client into a situation designed to ensure that she would break a leg on the eve of their departure to the exact place I wished to visit and at exactly the right time of year!'

'Oh, the poor woman . . .!' Conscience cast a troubled shadow over Cherry's blue eyes.

'Poor be damned!' Not for the first time, Cherry noted an edge of intolerance that hardened her friend's voice at every mention of the rich, privileged society whose members she seemed determined to emulate. 'Anyone who can afford the going rate for a place such as this,' she waved an encompassing hand around the luxurious bedroom, 'is certain to be promised an even more sumptuous holiday to make up for the minor mishap she's suffered. If you have sympathy to spare then spare some for me!' She finished, her dark eyes sparkling with indignation. 'Or think about yourself for a change! I know of no one more deserving of pity than a girl who's been compelled to leave her home, her mother, and a horde of younger brothers and sisters because of her stepfather's illogical dislike and jealousy of the strong bond of affection existing between herself and her mother! A girl who's pathetically grateful for having been given an opportunity to spend the rest of her working life behind the counter of a departmental store, a waif who was left floundering in a strange metropolis and who, had I not stumbled across her quite by chance, might eventually have met with some unspeakably gory end!'

Cherry's mouth trembled into a circle of protest, then suddenly widened into a smile that had a dimple of amusement tacked on to its edges.

'You're dramatising again, Diana,' she rebuked in a tone totally devoid of rancour 'I shall always feel grateful for the helping hand you extended at a time when I was desperately in need of a friend, but you must admit that our meeting was mutually beneficial. Must I remind you that prior to our first encounter you'd spent weeks searching for a congenial companion to share the expenses of your flat? Also,' knowing Diana's penchant for hugging the centre stage, she rushed to block an imminent interruption, 'far from feeling condemned to a life of servitude, I love selling perfume and can think of no other job that could tempt me away from the store.'

Predictably, Diana's hands rose in a gesture of dismay, but in spite of her obvious impatience and contempt of such aimless lack of ambition, there was resignation in her sigh.

'At first, I thought you were kidding when you told me that your mother always followed the example set by austere Puritans who insisted upon choosing names for their children from the Old Testament. I've no idea what effect such "abstract virtue" names have had upon your younger sisters, Faith, Prudence and Honour,' she shuddered fastidiously, 'but I'm becoming gradually convinced that your solemn, almost puritanical attitude towards life, your uncanny serenity and reluctance to believe ill of anyone, are virtues so rare to our generation they must have been willed into your soul by the quaintly pious mother who christened you Charity.'

Immediately the words were spoken Diana became aware that she had trespassed. Belatedly, she recalled Cherry's fierce loyalty towards those she loved, and also her ridiculous sensitivity about a name she disliked, not because of personal vanity, but because it had so often been used as a weapon of sarcasm, spat with venom from her stepfather's honed tongue.

Frantically she sought for words to heal the breach her brittle mockery had caused between herself and the girl whose expression bore a marked similarity to one she had seen while viewing a television programme that had made no conscious impact at the time—the look on the face of a seal cub whose friendly approach to the human who had invaded his territory had been answered with a mortal blow, and no reason why . . .

'Cherry, I'm sorry, I didn't mean . . .'

But for the first time in a two-year-long friendship during which Diana's cultivated flow of acid wit had often wreaked havoc on her victim, Cherry did not rush to meet her halfway.

'You promised, after I'd confided in you, never to refer to that subject again,' she accused in a flat, expressionless monotone so far removed from her usual happy lilt that Diana recognised it as a barometer registering a deep degree of hurt.

Intense shame, allied to frustration caused by plans that had moved nowhere near to fruition, combined to produce a typical flare of anger.

'Oh, get lost, Cherry!' she glared, spinning on her heel to stalk back into the bedroom. 'I wish I hadn't brought you to Cannes—you don't like it here, it's not your scene, you've made that very obvious by the wet-blanket attitude you adopted the moment we arrived! *It's not fair!*' she spun round to accuse her startled, wide-eyed friend. 'You must know how much this visit means to me, how much I long to break into films. For just one week in each year Cannes is packed solid with directors, producers, and talent scouts, all on the lookout for fresh new faces. Would-be starlets flock here from every corner of the globe, knowing that if they're fortunate enough to catch the right eye, excite the right attention, their names could be made! Given half an opportunity I *know* I could make it!' she exploded wrathfully. 'All I need is a break, a chance to impress some man of influence—but with you as my companion I haven't a hope in hell. In fact,' she almost spat the bitter taunt, 'your behaviour over the past few days has led me to suspect that you've deliberately set out to spoil my chances and that the motive behind your lack of co-operation is most likely jealousy!'

The accusation exploded like a bombshell inside the luxurious bedroom. Then followed an aftermath of stunned silence during which it seemed to Cherry that a yawning crater had opened up between herself and the girl whose kindness she had returned with the overflow of affection that had built up inside her since being deprived of its usual family outlet. Though she felt sickened, her stomach churning, she responded with quiet dignity.

'That simply is not true, Diana—I'm not implying that you possess no enviable assets,' she stumbled hastily, 'on the contrary, in spite of the fact that Cannes is bursting at the seams with the world's most beautiful girls, you can hold your own with the best of them. But if there's one lesson I've learnt over the past few years it is that it's no use aspiring to be an astronaut if one is scared of heights. You're brave, Diana, you deserve to reach the moon, but my hesitant feet will always stay planted on the ground. With your looks and personality you could marry a prince, whereas I,' her lips trembled into a wry smile, 'could live quite happily with a man as ugly as a toad provided he was prepared to offer me a home. My one ambition in life is to have my own home, my own children ... and a husband, of course,' she added almost as an afterthought. 'But your beauty deserves a special sort of setting,' she stated with a generosity that caused Diana to squirm. 'However, though I'd do anything within my capabilities to help you achieve your ambition, I'm afraid you're right in what you said,' she gulped. 'I'll always let you down because I'm such a dreadful actress, utterly incapable of playing a role.'

'You can say that again!' Rudely, Diana turned her back upon the girl whose sorrowful blue eyes were forcing her to feel an affinity with the merciless skinners of seal cubs, yet she carried on the row by tossing across her shoulder, 'You've reacted with distaste to every friendly male approach; stammered and blushed like a schoolgirl whenever a man has made a pass; declined every invitation without giving me time to vet the donors!'

'But the men who've asked us to dine with them have all been old!' Cherry gasped. 'It never once occurred to me that you'd want to spend time in the company of men old enough to be your father—horrible lecherous-looking men with bodies as rotund around the middle as the cigars they smoke!'

Diana tossed her head, mechanically adopting the stance she assumed when parading around the edge of the bathing pool wearing a microscopic bikini that exposed every flawless curve, a tiny waist, and long slender legs.

'Don't be a sentimental fool,' she simmered dangerously. 'I'd date the Hunchback of Notre Dame if I thought he could further my career! In Cannes, at present, good-looking men are ten a penny, but they too are interested only in finding a sponsor, someone who can mould and fire common clay into a scintillating starburst. Unfortunately,' she shrugged, 'such men are seldom physically appealing, but at this stage of the game sex appeal is not important—let's hope that kind of sport will follow later.'

Cherry stared, too shocked to speak, wondering

if Diana was serious or merely venting her frustration with meaningless bravado.

'Are you implying . . .?' She croaked, then cleared her throat and began again. 'I don't believe you're as ruthless and uncaring as you're attempting to appear, Diana. I *do* believe you when you say you'll do anything to break into films, even though you've deserted the recognised path of fame that leads from tea-girl to A.S.M. in rep, from bit parts to juvenile lead, then possibly to successful auditions. But whatever you may say, you'll never convince me that you're prepared to pay the price most film executives expect in exchange for their favours!'

When Diana remained silent, her body very still, Cherry found herself praying that her judgment was correct, that behind the liberated front she chose to hide behind Diana's morals remained intact. She held her breath as slowly Diana turned round to face her, then expelled it with relief at the sight of a familiar, slightly mocking smile.

'Please stop worrying about me, Cherry,' she teased as if harsh, accusing words had never been spoken. 'I don't mind placing emphasis upon sex appeal, or even contriving situations in which I can flaunt before the movie moguls wearing the minimum of clothing, but where I do draw the line is outside my bedroom door! I have no intention of falling into the same trap as many girls who flock to Hollywood hoping to make it as the new sensation, only to end up as just another writhing body in a skin-flick. All I want is a chance to demonstrate my acting ability,' she pleaded in deadly earnest. 'Promise me you'll co-operate,

Cherry! Please say you'll help me to get the break I need!'

Cherry swallowed hard, trying to steel her heart against the pathos being projected by eyes set like twin emeralds in an oval face with perfect features and a pale, flawless complexion carefully protected from the drying, wrinkle-inducing effect of the strong Riviera sunshine. She knew to her cost that Diana was a born actress, capable of switching from hard determination to melting tenderness, from friendship to enmity, from kindness to intolerance, with consummate ease. Nevertheless, in spite of her resolve to endure no more of the agonising embarrassment of the past few days, she felt her defences crumbling beneath the barrage of pleading being directed from soulful green eyes.

'I can understand your reluctance to be deprived of company because time is less inclined to drag when one has someone to talk to,' she blurted desperately, 'but I do so hate sitting in the coffee shop for hour after hour, attempting to make one very expensive drink last an infinity, while men parade past sizing up the possibilities of the goods on show, men whose salacious glances, flickering from one girl to the next, remind me of greedy children let loose in a sweet shop who are finding themselves spoilt for choice!'

'As I've already explained,' Diana countered tightly, obviously determined to contain her impatience, 'to see and be seen, to appear in all the right places at exactly the right time, is a recognised rule of the game.'

'The name of the game being *slave market*,' Cherry grimaced, then immediately wished the

words unsaid when Diana responded with instant
fire to the critical taunt.

'No,' she disclaimed with a glitter that could
have sliced through steel, 'the name of the game
being *ambition*! A slave is tied to one master; I'm
prepared to accept as many masters as there are
men who might prove useful to the furtherance of
my career.'

An hour later, her spirit beaten into submission
by decisive argument and by reminders of past
kindnesses that Diana had strung like a necklace
of obligations around her wilting neck, Cherry
began dressing for the nightmarish process known
as aperitif time, the exercise of drinking cocktails
before dinner, made fraudulent by the fact that
they had already dined on rolls and cold meat
purchased from a back-street delicatessen and
smuggled up to their bedroom inside an accom-
modating beachbag.

She frowned at her reflection in a mirror,
disliking the way smoke-grey chiffon laid emphasis
upon a waist rendered ultra-slender by an
uncharacteristic lack of appetite, deciding that the
rounded primness of white collar and cuffs lent a
choirboy solemnity to blue eyes staring wide with
apprehension from a small, heart-shaped face that
shame had drained bloodless. Biting hard into a
bottom lip that had begun to tremble, she turned
aside to pick up a hairbrush, then started
counting, mechanically as a dutiful child, the
number of strokes her mother had always insisted
were necessary to add lustre to a fine-spun, pale
gold skein of newly washed hair.

'Only three more days to go,' she murmured,
attempting to bolster her saddened spirits, 'not

counting the final day which will probably be spent packing before our journey to the airport— and then home! Surely just a further brief spell of luxurious imprisonment, idle chatter, unbearable traffic noise, and the humiliation of knowing yourself labelled a movie-mad starlet willing to sell body and soul for the chance of a screen test, can be borne if at the end of it Diana is forced to face the fact that tough, cynical, unimpressionable movie moguls are more interested in exploiting female companionship than they are in discovering fresh theatrical talent!'

Heaving a sigh of resignation, she laid down her hairbrush and moved out on to the balcony to await Diana's emergence from the bathroom. Averting her eyes from the multiple lanes of traffic streaming nose to tail along the illuminated Croisette, she gazed far out to sea, beyond the forest of masts rising above yachts cramming every spare inch of the pleasure-craft harbour; past the jewelled peninsula of Cap Ferrat to where sea lying dark and dense as ink formed the lonely Baie des Anges, an area that seemed to epitomise the peace and tranquillity she sought. Out there, perhaps, it might be possible to escape. Out there, she might find freedom from a worry she had been unable to share even with Diana—a fear almost— that had begun as a sense of unease, then graduated into a certainty that she was being stalked, hunted as a timid animal turned into an object of prey.

Her first intimation of being closely watched had come from a casual glance around the crowded hotel foyer on the day of their arrival. Feeling nervous and ill at ease in the midst of a

sophisticated clientele, she had shrunk into the
corner of a settee, wishing she could disappear
inside plump velvet cushions that might help to
deaden the sound of shrill feminine voices, male
bellows and brays, popping corks, and wave after
wave of synchronized chatter. Even Diana, seated
next to her, though busy expending charm and wit
upon a man with a promising aura of authority,
had felt her jerk of surprise, the sudden rigidity of
her limbs.

'Why are you staring across the room like a
hypnotised rabbit?' she had demanded crossly,
tossing a cursory glance across her shoulder.

'Am I? Sorry, I hadn't realised ...' she had
stammered, sweeping lashes low to break the
magnetic beam linking her startled gaze to dark,
piercing eyes projecting a look of keen interest
across the width of the foyer. Incredibly, because
men seldom paid her attention even when Diana
was not present, confrontations with the intimidat-
ing stranger became too frequent to be shrugged
off as merely coincidental. Each time she had
raised her eyes from a book, glanced over the rim
of a coffee cup, bridged the width of a swimming
pool, or scanned the perimeter of a crowded room
her eyes had collided with his, so that now she was
familiar with his sardonic glance, with the set of a
mouth that struck her as being far from kind ...

'Well, how do I look?'

When Diana's demanding voice jolted her back
to reality she spun on her heel to assure her with
typical generosity:

'Ravishing, of course. But then you always do.'

'Thank you,' Diana smiled, acknowledging the
compliment with the grace of a queen. 'Tonight,'

she breathed with certainty, 'could be my lucky night! Some instinct, a feeling in my bones, tells me that something momentous is about to happen. That's why I decided to wear my very best dress,' she confided eagerly. 'I was holding it in reserve for a special occasion, but then I thought, as nothing seems to be happening, why not try to *make* something happen!'

Uttering a trill of laughter, she twirled a full circle, then remained quite still so that Cherry could admire the rise and fall of a silk skirt light as thistledown and the colour of flame billowing and belling before settling around her ankles with an exotic sigh.

'It looks very expensive,' Cherry judged with a frown, wondering how Diana could possibly have stretched her salary far enough to accommodate the cost of a dress that made her slim beautiful body appear excitingly vibrant, licked with flame.

'It was. Although it hasn't been paid for yet,' she admitted with a shrug. 'But before you start scolding, Cherry,' she hastened to block the scandalised protest trembling upon her friend's lips, 'let me remind you of that trite but nevertheless well-proven theory that it's necessary to speculate in order to accumulate. As a born gambler, I regard this dress as my last throw of the dice—so no further argument, if you please, it's time for us to make our way downstairs where all the action is due to take place!'

Their hotel was the most noted of all the elegant hotels lining the Boulevard de la Croisette, a promenade made fabulous by rare perfume rising from flower-crammed gardens, tall palm trees, restaurants, night clubs and luxury shops facing directly on to the sea. It was *the* meeting place of all the famous and infamous; noted and notorious, well-known and unknown, who flocked to the Riviera each year during the height of the festival season. Nevertheless, in spite of the conglomeration of expensively tailored men relying upon jewel-bedecked wives to proclaim their status, glamorous stars of film and television, and beautiful young girls deliberately underdressed in order to excite attention, it seemed, to Cherry's intense embarrassment, that every head among the milling throng turned towards the staircase to watch Diana's flamboyant descent into the foyer.

Colour flooded her cheeks as, deliberately fading out of the spotlight, she trailed miserably in Diana's wake with lashes drooping low over hot cheeks, hands nervously clasped, wishing she was a bird that could fly upwards to seek anonymity among the ornate frescoes of a high domed ceiling, or even a mouse that could scuttle between innumerable feet towards the nearest small hole. The fact that all eyes were trained upon Diana, and the knowledge that compared with her magnificence she contrasted like a patch of grey shadow cast by the sun, did not relieve an agony of embarrassment that lasted until she stumbled down the last step and attempted to melt towards the fringe of an admiring crowd.

During Diana's brief moment of glory she would have been content to allow Cherry to disappear out of sight with her blessing, had it not been for the portly middle-aged man who made a bee-line in their direction.

'Diana, honey, do you recall your promise to have dinner with me one evening?' he drawled.

'I've a friend who'd like to meet you.' To Cherry's horror she saw his eyes swivel in her direction. 'How about your young friend making up a foursome?'

'What a lovely idea!' Simultaneously, Diana slipped one hand within the crook of the man's elbow and manacled the other tightly around Cherry's wrist.

'Cherry dear,' she glittered a warning to be co-operative. 'I'd like you to meet Marcus Holliday, the American film producer. Aren't you as thrilled as I am at the prospect of joining his party for dinner?'

Cherry's lips parted on a gasp of surprise. Since the day of their arrival Diana had expended considerable effort in an attempt to gain the attention of the cynical, cigar-chewing executive whose slit-narrowed eyes had seemed to linger once or twice as if assessing her potential before sliding past, apparently unimpressed. He had implied that their dinner engagement had been prearranged, but the invitation had come as a complete surprise to Diana, of that she felt certain. Obviously Marcus Holliday had become so spoiled with adulation it had not occurred to him that his conceited self-assurance might be rebuffed, his invitation turned down!

'I'm sorry . . .' she began on a proud, cool note that terminated in a pained gasp when Diana's pointed fingernails gouged into the soft flesh beneath her cuff. 'Oh!'

'What's wrong, gal?' Marcus Holliday eyed her sharply. 'You've gone kinda pale.'

'Nothing is wrong,' Diana smiled sweetly,' she's just a little overwhelmed. After all, it isn't every day that a famous film producer invites her to join him for dinner. Please lead the way, Marcus,' she urged. 'Cherry is as eager as I am to meet your friend.'

Surreptitiously, while Marcus was ushering them in the direction of the dining-room, Cherry searched her bag for a tissue to slip between her wrist and a white muslin cuff already stained by a tiny spot of blood. Diana could be ruthless towards anyone who threatened to get in her way, she reflected sadly, then shuddered, not so much from pain caused by sharp fingernails as from the shock inflicted by the vicious look Diana had employed as a warning not to spoil the opportunity she had schemed, waited, even prayed for . . .

'My friend insisted on going on ahead to ensure that the table he has reserved satisfies all his requirements,' Marcus explained, sounding impressed, albeit unwillingly, by the notion of anyone possessing sufficient temerity to question the efficiency of the hotel's supremely aloof head waiter. 'The guy you're about to meet demands very high standards,' he continued boasting— almost as if, Cherry mused, he and Diana were caught up in the same social climbing routine. 'He's accustomed only to the best and refuses to accept anything less than perfection!'

When they stepped over the threshold, the huge dining-room, lit only by soft pink light cast by lamps set in the centre of individual tables, was empty of all but a few late diners and two couples swaying to music issuing from the instruments of a small band of musicians seated on a dais adjacent to a circular dance floor. The majority of the floor space was filled with conventional tables, but as a waiter guided them forward Cherry became aware of dining booths set intimately in the shadows of the farthest wall.

As if anticipating their arrival, a man rose to his feet as they approached. She glimpsed a tall, elegant figure uncoiling from a chair and rising until a width of shoulders and a proud dark head became obscured by shadow. Prisms of light glancing from diamond-studded cuffs, an extended hand, lean, tanned, and bearing a heavily crested ring on one finger, were all she saw of their host until he acknowledged Marcus's introduction by bowing low enough to allow light cast from a lamp to illuminate saturnine features.

'Diana Dermot—Cherry Sweet!' Marcus began in a tone bordering on deference. 'May I introduce Monsieur Lucien Tarascon, Duc de Marchiel—Lucien to his friends!'

'Cherry . . . a simple yet charming name,' a cool, slightly accented voice mocked her startled rigidity, 'evocative of pink blossom, delicate scent, and the unmarred innocence of springtime. Was it vanity or merit that influenced your obviously personal choice of name, *mademoiselle*?'

She stared, too shocked to respond. But when he reached out to take her hand with the obvious intention of raising her frozen fingers to his lips she jerked away, reacting with the fear of cornered prey to the hunter whose dark watchful eyes had monitored her every movement throughout the last three traumatic days . . .

CHAPTER TWO

DIANA took her time deliberating over the choice of superb dishes offered by an impressive menu, making no attempt to hide the pleasure she was feeling at the prospect of enjoying her first real meal since their arrival in Cannes.

Breakfast, consisting merely of coffee or tea, croissants, butter and a fruit preserve, was the only meal provided by the hotel without any extra charge. So, because their budget was strictly limited, they had been forced to eat frugally, buying the cheapest food available from back-street *charcuteries*, reserving the bulk of their money for hours spent sitting by the swimming pool, in the hotel lounge, or in the exorbitantly expensive coffee shop.

'If you have not already done so, Diana,' their handsome host drawled, 'might I suggest that you try a dish that is a specialty of the nearby island of Corsica? *Pâté de merles* owes its rich, unusual flavour to ingredients gathered from mountain slopes made fragrant with the sweet-smelling bushes of the *maquis*—spirit of myrtle, juniper berries, and of course, the main constituent of the dish, tender blackbirds fattened on a surplus of berries.'

'Oh, yes, please!' Diana sparkled, her exotic taste appeased. 'That sounds very inviting!'

'And what about you, Cherry?' She felt his keen

eyes willing her to look in his direction. 'Shall I order a portion for you?'

'*No!*' Fanned-out lashes flew upwards to reveal eyes dark with revulsion, wide with fear of the autocratic man whom she had been forced to greet as a stranger but whose quizzical eyes, derisive mouth, and tanned, sabre-sharp features were stamped indelibly upon her mind. Confirmation that her intuitive dislike was justified made her even more nervous and ill at ease. Beneath a veneer of smooth sophistication was a cavity where his heart should have been; beyond the polite suggestion put forward to his guests she had recognised the cruel insensitivity of a mind that could contemplate with pleasure the sacrificial slaughter of timid, helpless creatures of the wild.

Across the width of a table bathed in light casting a roseate glow over starched linen, gleaming cutlery, and tulip-shaped glasses filled almost to the brim with sparkling champagne, his questing glance seemed to search her soul, delving, probing for the reason behind the expression of disgust she could not erase from pale, set features.

When the tip of Diana's tapered heel dug into her ankle Cherry winced, reminded of her promise to co-operate, to repay the debt owing to her friend.

'I must apologise, *monsieur*,' she husked miserably, 'but my appetite is poor. If you have no objection, I would prefer just a small piece of cheese, and an apple, perhaps.'

'Nonsense, Cherry!' Marcus sounded annoyed, as if their host's good humour was his main priority. 'It's unthinkable that you should spurn the experience of sampling typical dishes of a region that's almost unfairly blessed with high-quality ingredients and a surfeit of culinary skill. Why not try oysters with champagne? Or the chicken liver gâteau?'

'There's no reason why Cherry should feel obliged to eat if she does not feel inclined to do so, Holliday,' the Duc intervened smoothly. 'Appetite should be tempted but never forced. The pleasure of eating, in common with most sybaritic rites, is dependent upon hunger, temptation, or mere curiosity about the taste of the fare on offer.'

'Cherry always has to be different,' Diana frowned, jumping to Marcus's defence. 'As long as I've known her she's been one foot out of step with the rest of mankind.'

'Perhaps she is marching to a different drummer,' his amused glance returned to torment Cherry. 'Or then again, it could be that she is clever enough to have realised that nothing attracts the eye more than a single white rose in a field of poppies.'

'How well you've judged her, Lucien!' Diana trilled with a familiarity Cherry knew she herself would never dare emulate. 'And how clever of you to guess that Cherry is one of a solitary breed who would prefer to be alone even in paradise!'

Sensitive to the note of chagrin in Diana's voice, her resentment of being ousted from centre stage by a bit player normally relegated to the background, Cherry strove to restore the situation to normal. Realising that, in spite of a throat that felt constricted by an iron band, she would have to eat in order to subdue the minor commotion, she forced herself to meet eyes boring into her face with the keen, narrowed stare of a marksman judging the nature of his target.

'I've changed my mind, *monsieur*,' she gulped. 'I *will* have something more substantial to eat—but nothing too rich,' she amended, courage stumbling before a barrage of unnerving scrutiny. 'What . . . what do you suggest?'

'First of all,' he responded in a reproving drawl, 'I would suggest that you address me as Lucien. Then, as you appear to be in no hurry to eat, and because anticipation acts as a hone upon blunted appetite, I shall ask Jacques, the head chef, to begin preparing crêpes Suzette. By the time he is ready for the final ritual of flambéing the pancakes before your very eyes you will be sharing Eve's craving for forbidden fruit!'

Cherry blushed to the tips of her ears when a peal of unkind laughter confirmed that his slightly risqué remark had not been lost upon Diana.

'Cherry has been strictly indoctrinated against sexual indulgence by a pious Irish mother,' she jeered cruelly. 'She's even shocked by the sight of girls parading topless on the beaches—a sight taken very much for granted by visitors to Cannes, as I'm sure you'll agree, Lucien. Undoubtedly, she should have lived during the Victorian era when prudes fitted tin fig leaves to statues in museums!'

Swamped by an excess of tongue-tied embarrassment, Cherry buried tightly clenched fists in her lap and swept a thick screen of lashes downward, hoping to obscure the glint of tears welling into her eyes. She could not understand Diana's show of jealous antagonism. The success she had longed for seemed to be almost within her grasp—why then was she not concentrating all her wit and charm upon Marcus Holliday, the man whose influential patronage could be the rocket needed to launch her towards stardom, instead of striving to capture the attention of the spoiled aristocrat who responded to her venomous remarks in a tone edged with boredom?

'Perhaps Cherry shares the same opinion as myself, which is that simple nudity appears pure compared with the vulgarity of contrived nakedness.'

Cherry caught a sharp breath, taken unawares by the novelty of feeling championed. Not one of the males inside her tightly-knit family circle had considered her feelings important. Her brothers, aping the swaggering conceit of a father who treated his wife and daughters like slaves provided to cook, clean and pander to his every demanding whim, had used her as a butt for their insensitive humour, had even laughed without remorse when, as had frequently happened, her stepfather's resentful tongue had reduced her to tears.

She chanced a quick glance towards the Duc under half-lowered lashes and was caught, held fast by a thread of sympathy spun delicately as a web between them.

Taking pity upon her confusion, Lucien turned his attention upon the portion of pâté on his plate and began chatting easily, entertaining Marcus and Diana with a flow of amusing anecdotes that added to their enjoyment of many varied courses, each of which Cherry refused.

Relieved at being once more relegated to her customary place in the background, she sat quietly listening to the man who appeared to be intimately acquainted with every artist, banker, aristocrat and politician that formed the highly international clientele drawn to Cannes by its famous festivals. Casually, he discussed with Marcus the various leisure activities, displaying expert knowledge of sailing, golf, flying, scuba diving, and a bewildering variety of water sports. Not until a waiter distracted his attention by wheeling a trolley laden with cooking apparatus near to Cherry's elbow did he attempt to include her directly in the conversation.

Lifting her untouched glass of champagne from the table, he tipped the entire contents into the ice bucket.

'Let me pour you a fresh glassful. *Tiens*, I can think of no more disastrous marriage than that of crêpes Suzette and flat champagne! Have you heard the story behind the creation of our famous dish, *ma chérie*?' Without giving her time to recover from the shyness imposed by his deliberate slurring of her name into an endearment, he quizzed Diana.

'You are both English, are you not?' He looked pleased when she nodded. 'Ah, then you will be interested to learn that a member of your Royal Family is said to have been responsible for its creation—the heir to the throne of Queen Victoria, no less.'

Nodding acknowledgement of the appearance of a chef enveloped from his ankles to the tip of his tall domed hat in spotless white, Lucien waited, indulging Cherry's intense interest in the chef's almost theatrical display of expertise as he melted butter until it bubbled in a chafing dish heated by a small table burner, before pouring in half a small pitcher of mixed liqueurs which

immediately burst into flame. Encouraged by
Cherry's expression of awe, Jacques gestured
proudly as a magician about to perform a
favourite trick, then when the flames died down he
placed inside the chafing dish four small pancakes
folded into triangles, doused them with a sauce
blended from sugar and mixed orange and lemon
peel, then began basting until the pancakes were
thoroughly reheated and soaked in the citrus-
flavoured sauce. Much to Cherry's delight, he then
poured in the remaining liqueur and allowed it to
catch alight. Immediately the flames had died
down, he arranged the pancakes on a silver salver
and presented them to Cherry with a triumphant
flourish.

Eager to sample the outcome of such culinary
magic, and completely oblivious to her interested
audience, she forked a pancake on to her plate,
then transported a small portion to her lips.
Slowly, she savoured the featherlight, ambrosial
delicacy that Lucien had chosen especially to give
her pleasure.

'Mmm! They're heavenly, Jacques,' she assured
the anxiously hovering chef. Then, feeling
pampered as a princess she sampled another piece,
then another, until a peal of indulgent laughter
made her hesitate with her fork in mid-air, a rosy
blush racing into her cheeks.

'No need to stop, *chérie*,' Lucien teased,
seemingly much amused by her unrestrained
enjoyment, but then spoiled her appetite by adding
a trifle cynically. 'While most beautiful girls find it
easy to get what they want from life, only the
wisest manage to actually enjoy the fruits of their
scheming!'

She cast a swift, puzzled look in his direction, then quickly switched her attention to her plate. But her sweet dish of pleasure had been spoiled, soured by the dash of contempt she had recognised in the tone of the man who exuded world-weary sophistication like an exclusive cologne.

As if Diana, too, had felt the prick of his cynicism upon her conscience, she hastened to change the subject.

'You didn't finish explaining our Prince's connection with the creation of crêpes Suzette,' she reminded him brightly. 'I'm aware that Queen Victoria's son languished for years in his mother's shadow, but surely you were not about to tell us that a man of his station was forced to exorcise boredom by working in some kitchen?'

'Hardly.' Cherry felt the weight of his brooding eyes lift from her bent head when politeness compelled him to respond to Diana's prompting. 'I make no claim for the story's authenticity, even though an ancestor of mine was said to have been one of several friends chosen to lunch with the Prince at the Café de Paris in Monte Carlo some time during the late nineteenth century.

'The party was made up of gentlemen and a young actress whose name was Suzette. The chef, in honour of the Prince's patronage, had devised a special sauce based upon a simple dish favoured by his own peasant family. But as so often happens in the presence of royalty, nervousness made the young chef clumsy, consequently, as he stood near the Prince's table reheating the pancakes in his newly-created sauce, flames reached the liqueurs and set the whole pan alight.

'In spite of the disaster, the Prince politely

insisted that the pancakes should be served. Apprehensively, the Prince and his companions tried the pancakes, then began spooning up the sauce, which they declared was delicious.

'"What name have you given to this superb pudding?"' the Prince enquired.

'Immediately, the astute young chef replied:

'"None, as yet, Your Highness. But I would deem it a great honour if you would allow me to christen the sweet in your name?"

'The Prince declined the honour, but gallantly insisted that the name chosen should be that of the only lady present. The much flattered girl jumped to her feet and holding her skirts wide, dropped him a deep curtsey.

'"I dub this pudding crêpes Suzette!" the Prince clowned mockingly, tapping the tip of his knife lightly on each of her shoulders. "Arise, exquisite dish of fire and flame—sweet, saucy, and deliciously satisfying!"'

In spite of an inner voice urging her to remain aloof, Cherry's eyes were drawn as if magnetised to stare across the table at features made to look saturnine by deep shadows cast where rays from a pink globe of light could not reach. As slowly she traced the course of thick black eyebrows scored over eyes rendered dark and hard as agate, across a taut sweep of jaw and lips that had once again reverted to displaying the sardonic twist which she had begun to recognise as his trademark, she felt a well of panic and fear rising up inside of her. It hardly seemed possible that a man of such distinction, a rich nobleman capable, even in this playground of the world's most beautiful people, of turning every female head, should find her

remotely interesting. Yet instinct, allied to the
silent persecution he had imposed since the day of
her arrival, told her that their meeting had been
deliberately manipulated, that for some unac-
countable reason he had persuaded Marcus to use
his slight acquaintanceship with Diana as a bridge
towards a formal introduction.

She shivered, reluctant to even consider becoming once more hostage to a man's unreasonable
claims. How the situation would have appealed to
Ryan's warped sense of humour! How her
stepfather would have laughed at the notion of his
puritanical stepdaughter—who had found it impossible to hide her disgust of his constant
womanising—being hunted, stalked and finally
cornered by a man who had obviously appraised
her character, reached a verdict, and judged her
virtues deserving of the same reward as that
bestowed upon a flirtatious actress by her
aristocratic patron . . .

Betraying the fact that he knew nothing of
history and cared even less, Marcus reacted like a
man inspired.

'Say, that would make a great screen scenario,
Lucien! Prince meets beautiful showgirl, becomes
entranced by her charm, and in spite of
scandalised opposition from his family presents her
at Court as his future bride! We'd have to have a
well-known actor as leading man, of course, but
his female counterpart would need to be completely
unknown, preferably an English girl with sufficient
talent to project the sweet, dewy-eyed look of
innocence even actresses seemed to possess in the
olden days.'

His eager glance swept around the table, noting

Diana's look of startled anticipation, Cherry's appalled wince, and Lucien's closed-down, totally unreadable features.

'I know you're gonna tell me that it's all been done before, but,' Marcus jutted his chin to lend emphasis to his argument, 'I'm willing to gamble on a revival of public interest in the classic costume romantic melodrama. What you have to bear in mind is the public's insatiable greed for nostalgia, the need to be transported, if only for a couple of hours, out of the modern-day world with its constant threat of warfare, its promiscuity, and daily acts of violence. Take my word for it, period movies are acknowledged box office hits—happiness pills gulped down by millions even without the syrup of an extensive hype campaign!'

He leant back in his seat, flushed with the fire of his own rhetoric, and waited for his words to sink in. But when no immediate reaction was forthcoming he leant across the table to prompt:

'Well, Lucien, you promised to back my next picture, are you still agreeable?'

Cherry tensed, hoping Lucien's refusal would be tactfully phrased, that he would not hurt Marcus's feelings by laughing him to scorn. But to her utter disbelief, he responded in a quiet, even thoughtful, tone.

'I am willing to be guided by your knowledge of the film industry, Holliday, and I know you well enough to feel certain that you would not participate in any venture likely to put your hard earned reputation at risk. So ...' his hesitation was slight, nevertheless, Cherry sensed that some message of great import was about to be transmitted, '... provided the unknown girl chosen to star in the film meets with our mutual approval, I see no reason to withhold agreement.'

Cherry wondered whether a trick of light had led her to imagine the almost imperceptible flicker of Lucien's eyes in Diana's direction. But when Marcus, as if prompted by a cue, turned a beam of approval upon her obviously excited friend Cherry's hackles rose to a scent of collusion in the air. She felt a sudden surge of fear for Diana, who was sitting with her hands tightly clasped, barely able to contain her delight, obviously sharing none of her own suspicions that she had been singled out as a likely pawn in some deliberately contrived chess game.

She felt her sense of unease was justified when Marcus stated with suave complacency:

'Then we have a deal, Lucien! My one and only stipulation, so far as our prospective leading lady is concerned, is that she should be a novice, completely unknown to the public, but with the looks and figure expected of a movie star. I'd class a talent for acting as a gratuitous rather than essential asset,' he boasted unpleasantly. 'So far, every bird I've handled has soared straight to stardom on *my* wings!'

Lucien nodded acknowledgement, then as if anxious to forestall any further comment, rose to his feet and bowed before Cherry.

'Will you permit me the pleasure of dancing with you, *ma chère*?'

A swift glance towards the dance floor where tightly embracing couples stood swaying, their feet almost motionless, was sufficient to inspire a horrified refusal.

'Come!' In spite of her stiff resistance he insisted

upon levering her to her feet. 'This is no time for mock modesty—you must know that I find you intriguing, that there are questions I must ask that only you can answer.'

Normally, she was slow to be moved to anger. But the sting of his derisive whip smarted her head high with pride. She too, had questions waiting to be asked, fears to be allayed, even if the price she had to pay was close proximity to the only man who could supply the answers.

'Very well, *monsieur*.' Displaying a dignity that provoked a gleam of admiration into his watchful eyes, she jerked out of his clutches and began gliding gracefully as a boneless grey ghost in the direction of the dance floor.

But her mood of defiance lasted only until his hands slid around her waist, then upwards along her spine until his palms were lying flat against each shoulderblade, pinning her close enough to feel every sinewed movement of his muscular chest, narrow hips, and insidiously pressing thighs.

In spite of a sheltered upbringing she had not remained totally removed from male advances, but the fumbling passes she had suffered at the hands of teenage dancing partners, their hesitant attempts to combine slap and tickle with the furtherance of a schoolday acquaintanceship, had in no way prepared her for her first encounter with the amatory tactics of a very experienced philanderer.

'*Vous avez un de ces corps, c'est incroyable, mon ange!*' he murmured seductively, feathering his lips across one pink, fiery lobe.

She felt his spasm of silent laughter rippling inside her as if, being held so closely, they had become one—one body, one heart, one mass of singing veins, pounding nerves, and wildly responsive flesh.

'Your reaction tells me that you understood my compliment, *ma chère*, but surely you are not half so shocked as you appear, others beside myself must have told you that you have an incredible body.'

Goaded into action by his physical and mental torture, she jerked a foot of space between them and managed to force an outraged whisper.

'What devious game are you playing? Why did you and Marcus deliberately lead Diana to hope that she might be chosen as the film's leading lady—before any other actresses have been auditioned and without having had so much as a screen test?'

Giving her no time to continue her whispered onslaught, he snapped a hand around her wrist and hustled her off the dance floor towards a door giving access to a deserted terrace. Cherry felt the solidity of a stone balustrade against her spine when he released her to stare down at her moon-stroked features, his expression registering cynical resignation.

'I must admit to having been prepared for some sign of chagrin, but not for such lack of finesse! Not once, during days spent monitoring your behaviour, have I seen you betray such a lamentable lack of composure. It is to be hoped,' he astonished her, 'that I shall never be called upon to do so again.' Seemingly unaware that she had been rendered speechless, he shrugged. 'Perhaps I am partly to blame for your jealous outburst—I may have been too cautious, spent too much time observing your actions without bothering to explain my motives. But I wanted to be absolutely certain that you were suitable, that you possessed all the necessary characteristics, before broaching the proposition I have in mind.'

'Proposition . . .?' she echoed weakly. Then, as the word rang an ominous note in her mind, she croaked:

'Are you actually *admitting* that you've been spying on my movements day and night since my arrival in Cannes? *Why* . . .?' How dare you keep watch on me as if I were some sort of . . . of . . . *threatened species*!'

'Wasn't that your exact aim?' he glinted coldly, 'to be seen to be different, to make the *crowd* stand out from around *you*? You must have been perfectly well aware that mine were not the only flame-dazzled eyes drawn to rest upon a pale undecorated candle. Who else but an extremely clever person would choose to dress like a Quaker marooned in the Garden of Eden; would calculate that a tightly stretched tee-shirt and skimpy shorts could excite a man's interest far quicker than the nudity we have become accustomed to seeing draped around bathing pools, or would train her voice to a husky pitch that falls sweet as the call of a Lorelei upon ears deafened by a competitive screech of conversation? Yes, *chérie*, after hours of careful scrutiny, there is no doubt in my mind that you are a talented and extremely intelligent actress.'

'I am . . .?' Cherry blinked.

'Most certainly,' he nodded. 'Exactly the person I need to act out a role calling for quick wits, dedication, and an ability to perform without a blush should circumstances ever warrant a bold display of hypocrisy.'

CHAPTER THREE

'TELL me again exactly what Lucien said!'

With a shiver of dread, Cherry tried to escape a further attempt by Diana to browbeat her into submission by tipping her sunhat forward so that its wide brim cast an obscuring shadow over eyes that responded with a leap of shock to the mere mention of the Duc de Marchiel. Striving to project an air of indifference, she forced stiff limbs to relax against the mattress laid out on the stony stretch of beach reserved for the exclusive use of guests of the hotel rearing skyward beyond a strip of flower-massed boulevard.

'I've repeated his proposition verbatim almost a dozen times and I refuse to do so again,' she declined, forcing a bored yawn. 'Please, Diana, let's drop the subject, try to relax and enjoy this glorious sunshine.' Determined to change the subject, she raised a bare, gold-toasted leg in the air and heaved a disappointed sigh.

'Hmm ... not exactly the Riviera tan my workmates will be expecting! Still, now that the Festival is over and the film moguls are preparing to move out, we shall be able to devote the rest of our holiday entirely to sunbathing.'

'Yes, and you'd be perfectly content to do just that, wouldn't you!' Cherry's hopes died, shrivelled by the heat of Diana's blazing scorn. 'Well,' she continued sharply, 'you may be prepared to return home with only a tan to remind you of an

opportunity of a lifetime, but I most certainly
am not!' Shaking with temper, Diana stood up
to fling a sarong-type beach robe over her bikini.
'I'm going to find Marcus, to *beg* him to take
me with him when he flies back to the States
tomorrow!'

The defiant threat jolted Cherry upright to stare,
aghast as a schoolgirl by her friend's daring.

'Diana, you can't! Marcus has made you no
promises—a few dropped hints and suggestive
glances, yes—but no definite guarantee that he's
prepared to groom you for stardom!'

'And don't *dare* to pretend that you don't know
why!' Stooping to glower beneath the fringe of a
beach umbrella lodged into the shingle between
their mattresses, Diana raised a bitter look over
Cherry's modest one-piece bathing suit. 'Lucien
has made it quite plain to Marcus that unless you
agree to co-operate the deal between them is off.
The Lord alone knows why he should have chosen
you—in spite of the incredible amount of talent
available—to help him out of his difficulties!
Either he sees something in you that others don't,
or he's mistakenly endowed you with qualities that
don't exist!'

'I hope the latter.' Cherry tried hard to keep the
hurt she was feeling out of her voice when she
defended quietly: 'It's hardly flattering to be
considered capable of playing a lying, deceitful,
hypocritical role, even when the package comes
wrapped in the guise of employment.'

'Oh, for heaven's sake! All Lucien did was offer
a few weeks' work to a girl he assumed was an
out-of-work actress, offer you a chance to act in a
drama that has nothing to do with truth but is

pure makebelieve, a medium designed to free people from the pressures of reality!'

Fearing reason was in danger of being swept aside by passionate rhetoric, Cherry reminded her friend swiftly:

'What you appear to have forgotten, Diana, is that I am not, nor have I ever wanted to be, an actress! And besides, what do you suppose my boss's reaction would be were I to saunter into the store a couple of months from now with the object of taking up my job where I'd left off? What possible reason could I give to explain my prolonged absence?'

Diana shrugged. 'Tell him by telegram that you have resigned. The fee Lucien has offered to pay for your services would keep you in comfort for a year at least—ample time in which to find alternative employment.'

Cherry drew a sharp breath. 'I couldn't do that even if I wanted to, and I certainly don't!' she jerked.

Diana leant forward until her brilliant green stare was levelled directly upon Cherry's apprehensive face.

'Not even,' she queried in a voice silken with threat, 'if I were to tell you that if you do return home you'll have to find some other place to live, that the door of my flat will be permanently closed to you?'

Cherry stared back dumbly, shaken by a depth of vindictiveness she had never dreamt existed. She blinked, then turned her head aside, pretending that the glare of sunlight upon brilliant blue water was responsible for a need to brush an unsteady hand over tear-spiked lashes.

'You don't mean that, Diana,' she husked through a tightly closed throat. 'I know how desperately you want to break into films, how you've even begun to regard me as a stumbling block in the way of cherished ambitions, nevertheless our friendship has to mean something—two years of scrimping and sharing, laughing and crying, rejoicing and commiserating with one another can't be wiped from your mind as if they'd never existed!'

'No,' Diana agreed calmly, 'but they can be ignored for as long as it takes me to forgive your deception.'

'Deception . . .?' Cherry faltered, looking totally bewildered.

'Indeed, yes,' Diana confirmed, her eyes a hard, unforgiving green. 'You claim to be talentless, yet only a consummate actress could have managed to keep hidden for so long the hard core of selfishness that was suddenly revealed when, for the first time in our acquaintanceship, you were called upon to put the welfare of others before that of your own. But perhaps I could be doing you an injustice.' Diana frowned, seeming momentarily uncertain. 'Is it possible, Cherry, that you've never given serious thought to the number of people who, through no fault of their own, have become greatly dependent upon your charity?'

'Upon *my* charity?' Fleetingly, the thought crossed Cherry's mind that Diana was expert at reducing her to a mumbling mass of humility. Yet it was a relief to see her brow clear, to hear words of genuine warmth issuing from lips that had melted suddenly into lines of smiling compassion.

'Cherry dear,' Diana dropped down on the

mattress beside her, 'did you *really* think that I'd been pleading my own solitary cause?' She waited, her head cocked to one side, as if hoping to hear a denial, then breathed softly: 'I do believe . . .!' Quickly, looking anxious to redeem a wrong, she began enumerating. 'Firstly, there's Lucien, who seems adamantly certain that you're the only person who can help sort out his problem. Secondly, Marcus is dependent upon Lucien's backing, which will only be forthcoming if you agree to co-operate. Then last but most importantly, there are the hundreds of film extras who, like myself, are badly in need of employment—to say nothing of camera crews and scores of studio technicians. Just think of the employment to be gained from a new film, Cherry—the new sets that would have to be designed, new songs to be written, new costumes to be made, dances to be choreographed, hair-styles to be created, make-up——'

'Stop, please stop!' Appalled by the sudden application of a weight of responsibility, Cherry protested: 'You're not being fair, Diana. You've no right to make me feel bound by obligations that haven't been freely accepted!'

For a second it seemed certain that Diana was about to revert to the hard, angry attitude she had adopted the evening before when, after leaving Marcus, she had walked into their room and found Cherry pacing furiously, anxious to confide her shocked indignation and downright disgust of Lucien Tarascon's outrageous proposition. She braced for further argument when Diana sat back on her heels, her green eyes glittering hard as the emeralds she was determined one day to own.

Then to Cherry's relief, Diana's tightly pursed
mouth relaxed to allow her full bottom lip to
assume its customary winsome pout.

'Of course you're right, Cherry dear,' she
confessed, smiling sadly into blue eyes stunned by
the novelty of hearing Diana admit, for the first
time ever, that she was wrong. 'You're perfectly
entitled to give your own interests primary
consideration. Forget about me, or about Marcus
and the rest of the eager hopefuls.' Slowly she rose
to her feet, then bent to pick up a beachbag,
heaving a dejected sigh. 'We'll cope, somehow or
other we'll get by . . .'

After Diana had disappeared in the direction
of the hotel Cherry sank back on to the mattress
fighting an urge to cry. She had no reason to
feel guilty, she assured herself, turning on her
stomach to rest her aching head on an outflung
arm. Closing her eyes, she tried to blot out a
scene of happy activity that was only serving to
intensify her misery—girls no older than herself
with bared breasts nut-brown to the nipples
proclaiming them members of the local élite,
chatting in companionable groups yet keeping
watchful eyes upon the bevy of naked, frolicking
infants milling around them. And upon their
even more darkly tanned husbands, lithe young
men—every one a broad-shouldered, narrow-
hipped Adonis—wearing brief shorts belted
around flat midriffs, some swimming, some
lazing in the sun, some perfecting their technique
on windsurfing boards, others merely to-ing and
fro-ing between the beach and the bar restaurant
at the rear of the *plage*, but each without
exception displaying the confident, élitist swagger

of a rich, privileged sun-god perfectly at home in his environment.

She stirred restlessly, disturbed by the intrusion into her thoughts of a presence that served as a reminder that there existed a serpent in every paradise, a man who, because he had been reared in the rarified atmosphere of power, wealth and privilege, had been astonished by her refusal to pander to his whim.

In spite of her resolve not to dwell upon her last encounter with Lucien Tarascon, his compelling personality surfaced vengeful as a sea god through waves of thought, towering until his incensed, black-browed expression filled the entire horizon of her mind. All sound around her seemed to fade, even the constant roar of traffic streaming along the boulevard above became drowned by the recollection of Lucien's confident, pleasantly modulated voice outlining his plans for her future.

There had been just one huge star twinkling through the dark blue mantle cast by midnight over the deserted bay. Except for themselves the terrace had been deserted. Leaves of palm trees lining the Croisette far below had hung heavily in the still air, yet the scent of banked-up roses, of thyme sharing beds with stately irises, had combined with the hot red tang of geraniums to tease her senses, made her lightheaded enough to wonder at first if Lucien, too, had been so much affected that he had begun talking nonsense.

'I have a problem to confide, *chérie*,' he had begun, then without further preamble had launched into a clipped commentary. 'My cousin Claudine is very dear to me. As she is some years older than myself, her attitude when we were children was always tender and protective, so much so that she gradually began to represent the sister I had never had, the mother I had never known. She married young. Naturally,' he had smiled fondly, 'such treasures as she are not allowed to remain buried for long. I was barely fifteen when Mistral, her only child, was born.'

In spite of her bewilderment Cherry had listened patiently—still a little bemused by the few sips of champagne he had insisted she must try—and had not intruded with speech even when he had lapsed into silence, staring out to sea as if deeply immersed in thought. Just when, unnerved by his prolonged silence, she had begun searching her mind for some excuse to leave him alone, he had resumed speaking, more rapidly this time, as if trying to keep pace with racing thoughts.

'Claudine's husband, Pierre, is a member of the French Diplomatic Corps—a career that entails much travelling and living for a few years at a time in many different countries. The problem of Mistral's education was solved at first by employing governesses, then tutors if no suitable school was available. When she reached the age of twelve, however, her mother began fretting that her daughter might be missing out, so, after installing her in a boarding school in Paris, she begged me to offer her a home during the vacations. Though unwilling, I felt I could not refuse. Yet in spite of my misgivings the arrangement has worked out surprisingly well—until recently.'

His frown had darkened into a definite scowl.

'Mistral, now a precocious seventeen-year-old, will shortly be leaving finishing school and returning to live with her parents, but meanwhile, during vacations, she has become eager to sample the delights offered by our Riviera playground. Naturally, I could not allow her to do so unescorted, so, mindful of the duty I owe to her parents, I began escorting her myself—only to discover,' his lips had twisted wryly, 'that in common with most females, the more she is given, the greedier she becomes.'

At this point, Cherry had been moved to protest about this slur against her sex, but as if impatient to conclude an explanation he seemed to find aggravating, he had ignored her look of outrage and encapsulated what remained of his narrative into a few brief sentences.

'As a consequence of our constant appearances together at various functions and popular places of entertainment, we became the target of the *paparazzi*, pestilential cameramen who descend upon our coast each summer like a plague of insatiable locusts, and of gossip columnists who, in spite of being aware that Mistral and I are closely related, were unable to resist including in their rag-bag of malicious scandal dropped hints and sly innuendoes that have put her reputation very much at risk.'

He had paused as if willing, at this stage, to allow her to comment, but except for one fleeting spasm of envy of a girl nearing her coming of age without ever having had to work for a living, her mind had been rendered completely blank. Belatedly, because he had seemed to have been expecting sympathy, perhaps, for his need of a safety valve, some sympathetic and anonymous ear into which he could pour out his troubles, she had stammered a meaningless platitude.

'How . . . how embarrassing for you!'

'Exactly!' He had pounced upon her words with a satisfaction she had found startling at the time but which, in retrospect, she had compared to the simmering prelude to a volcanic eruption. 'Especially now that Mistral's head has been turned so much by non-stop publicity that she has actually begun to believe that she is in love with me! That is also the reason why I have been searching for someone as clever as yourself to act out the part of my fiancée for the next couple of months!' he had astounded her with an explosive rush of words. 'Perhaps now, you will realise how necessary it was for me to study your movements, to assess your character, to monitor your reactions to every given situation—and why I had to bribe Marcus with a promise of financial backing for his next movie in exchange for manoeuvring you into accepting an invitation to dine so that I could examine at close quarters the extent of your acting ability! You have passed every test with flying colours, *mademoiselle*!' His congratulations had sounded genuinely sincere. 'Few actresses of your tender age, however experienced, would choose to imitate Tennyson's description of pure innocence in front of such a cynical, world-weary audience, much less possess the ability to communicate its message with such conviction that even I have been tempted to believe in the survival from childhood of: *'That thrice happy state again to be,'* he had quoted whimsically. *'The trustful infant on the knee, Who lets his rosy fingers play About his mother's neck and knows Nothing beyond his mother's eyes'.*

Cherry twisted her body round until she was

lying flat on the mattress, wincing from probing further into the blistering exchange of words that had followed immediately she had managed to wrench strangled vocal chords out of the clutch of intense shock.

Had she really dared to storm at the imperious Duc de Marchiel? To call him an arrogant fiend, a cynical manipulator, a conceited, blackmailing despot, as well as a variety of milder yet no less contemptuous names?

Impatient with herself for allowing her mind to dwell upon a scene that made her feel agitated and unbearably cheapened, she jerked upright and twisted round to prop a backrest under one end of the mattress, then relaxed to resume her sunbathing in a half-reclining position. Because she and Diana had, through necessity rather than inclination, earned themselves a reputation among the *plage* attendants of being frugal tippers, their mattresses were invariably positioned to the rear of the beach—the stretch nearest to the sea being exclusively reserved for customers guaranteed to demonstrate their appreciation with hard cash. Consequently, in order to catch a glimpse of frolicking swimmers, Cherry was forced to crane her neck to peer above the heads and shoulders of the occupants of three rows of mattresses laid out in front of her own.

In the process of stretching and ducking over and under the outsized sunhat being worn by one of a party of Dutch holidaymakers sitting directly in front of her, she stiffened, then scrambled up on to her knees to stare long and hard in the direction of two mattresses set a little apart from the rest, almost at the water's edge, one occupied by a laughing young girl wearing a poppy-red swimsuit and a straw boater sporting a single large flower matching exactly the vivid lipstick smeared across a wide, generous mouth, and the other by a man whose teak-tanned shoulders were turned towards her but whose satanically dark, finely-sculptured head—even though damp and tousled by a recent swim—she would have recognised anywhere.

Even as she stared, petrified by the sight that had turned her limbs to stone, the dark-haired man swerved his head aside to dodge an errant beach ball, and his amused eyes swivelled to follow its progress as it was punched and patted by playful hands straight in her direction. Instinctively her reflexes responded as the ball soared towards her, and although her last intention was to join in the affray, seconds later she became the focus of the attention of an amused crowd applauding her dexterous capture of the ball she had clasped between her palms.

Blushing furiously, she tossed the ball back to its youthful owner, then in a panic-stricken rush began gathering up her things, keeping her back turned to the sea as she measured the distance between herself and the flight of stone steps leading up to the boulevard that had suddenly assumed the aspect of an escape route. She was all set to flee, had just slipped an arm into the sleeve of the short towelled robe that did double duty on the beach and in the bathroom, when a shadow fell across her face, causing her to shiver as if a dark patch of cloud had enveloped the sun.

She swung her head round and looked up,

straight into the impassive face of Lucien
Tarascon.

'You are leaving so soon, *mademoiselle*?' His
sharp glance raked the cleared mattress, her
haphazardly stuffed beachbag.

'Y-yes,' she stammered, casting around wildly in
her mind for some valid and believable reason. 'I'd
love to stay longer, but as I'm not yet acclimatised
to the heat I try to resist the temptation to spend
too many hours in the sun.'

'You have had your lunch?' With his keen eyes
daring her to lie she had no recourse but to
mumble:

'Not yet, but . . .'

'Then I insist that you join us.' Smoothly, he
slid a hand under her elbow and began propelling
her in the direction of a vine-covered pergola
where tables had been set and waiters were
hovering, eager to begin serving lunches. 'This
would appear to be an ideal opportunity for you
to meet my ward.' Calmly ignoring her gasp of
protest, he steered her towards a table. 'She has
been spoiled, that one!' Moodily, he shooed an
inoffensive kitten out of his path. 'Far from being
content to enjoy the facilities of our own private
beach, she insists that it is too quiet and managed
to persuade me that a day spent in the *plage* would
be a good idea. But half an hour spent in this
overcrowded playpen was sufficient to endear me
even more strongly to solitude. I'm afraid I've
been very poor company for the child, so perhaps,
mademoiselle,' his stiffly formal manner of address
was a certain indication of the depth of the
displeasure she had aroused during their last
meeting, 'the company of someone nearer her own

age will make up to Mistral for my somewhat
disgruntled attitude.'

After a table in a secluded corner of the terrace
had been vetted and designated suitable, Lucien
left her alone for the few minutes it took him to
escort his deserted ward from the beach. But
immediately she was introduced to the girl whose
flamboyant mouth had adopted a petulant droop,
Cherry sensed that however ungracious Lucien's
manner might have been, Mistral was disposed to
regard their luncheon guest as an unwelcome
intruder.

'*Bonjour, mademoiselle,* how kind of you to join
us,' she acknowledged with the barest civility
before turning dark, reproachful eyes upon
Lucien. 'You promised we would lunch at the
Negresco in Nice! You know how much I enjoy
being waited upon by flunkies dressed in knee-
breeches and silken hose, bright red jackets with
polished buttons, and silver-buckled shoes!'

'Not today, *petite*, some other time perhaps . . .'
With a snap of impatience Cherry found appalling,
Lucien dismissed the promise he must obviously
have made.

The effect upon his ward was devastating.
Childishly, because in spite of her chic appearance
Cherry felt certain that emotionally she was very
immature, Mistral's hurt mouth began quivering
and two huge teardrops appeared shimmering on
the brink of long, heavily mascaraed lashes.

Hastily, while Lucien's vexed glance was trained
upon the menu, Cherry threw her a lifeline.

'I feel so hot and sticky,' she sighed. 'I wonder,
Mistral, would you mind very much showing me
the way to the washroom?'

Mistral's grasp of the excuse she needed to avoid incurring a further show of male wrath was swift but stiffly ungracious.

'Volontiers, mademoiselle.' She stood up and, keeping her tear-stained cheeks carefully turned away from Lucien, instructed: 'Please follow me . . .'

The washroom, lined from floor to ceiling with embossed bronze tiles, had a range of chocolate brown basins with gold-plated fittings set into a vanitory unit running the length of one wall. Immediately they stepped inside an attendant appeared, proffering tiny coin-sized tablets of scented soap and pale yellow hand towels. Mistral waved her away, but Cherry made full use of the facilities offered.

A short while later, refreshed by her wash, she glanced upward while patting her face dry and went very still, her questioning eyes locked with Mistral's tearful stare reflected in a bronze-tinted mirror.

'I have admitted to Lucien that I am in love with him,' Mistral confessed with a childish honesty strangely at odds with a body transmitting a strong suggestion of maturity from behind the folds of a chic, expensive beachrobe. 'He insists that I am too young to have reached such a momentous decision, too immature to know my own mind.' She swallowed back tears with obvious difficulty. 'When he first began talking about a girl he had met, dined and fallen in love with all in the space of one evening, I felt certain she was just a figment of his chivalrous imagination, a ploy dreamt up perhaps with some notion of being cruel to be kind. I refused to listen to him praising your virtues, refused even to believe in your existence, because I felt certain that no one who does not know him as well as I do could possibly have persuaded him to abandon his bachelor status. I am still convinced that he will never marry you, *mademoiselle* . . .'

Hastily, Cherry recommenced patting her cheeks dry, unable to meet eyes liquid with adolescent suffering, yet unwilling to speak words that would confirm Mistral's earlier suspicion, thereby rendering her once more vulnerable to Lucien's far from certain temper.

But when Mistral continued speaking she stiffened, experiencing the shocked incredulity of one confronted by a kitten that has suddenly developed a man-hungry growl'

'Lucien has often fallen in love, but his passion has never outlasted the first far-off peal of wedding bells. Only I know exactly how to handle him! When I was merely twelve years old I decided that Lucien and I would marry, and so far,' her derogatory glance flicked Cherry's vanity on the raw, 'nothing has happened to make me change my mind. He pretends to be blind, refuses to admit that I am no longer a child,' she stressed dramatically, 'therefore your arrival on the scene is fortuitous, *mademoiselle*, inasmuch as your presence will serve as a constant reminder that I must work harder and faster to convince Lucien that I am fully grown up and very much in love with him!'

CHAPTER FOUR

When they rejoined Lucien on the terrace it was no surprise to Cherry to discover that, with typical arrogance, he had ordered without waiting to consult their wishes. Politely, he rose to his feet until she and Mistral were seated, then immediately signalled the waiter to begin serving.

'Have you tried *bouillabaisse* yet, *ma chérie*?'

Cherry's colour was heightened by the endearment he seemed to have adopted as a permanent form of address. Keeping her attention trained upon what appeared to be an excellent thick soup being ladled on to her plate, she sniffed appreciatively.

'Not yet. Does it taste as good as it smells?'

'Even better,' he assured her, looking well pleased. 'No visitor to France should ever leave without enjoying the experience of eating our famous fish stew, don't you agree, Mistral?'

When she did not respond he jabbed a look of impatience at a mouth trembling with petulance, at an expression downcast as a child who has been forced to forgo a promised treat.

Visibly aggravated by his condemning glance, Mistral snapped in defiance. 'No, I do not! It has a taste that may appeal to tourists and peasants, but personally I have no stomach for such glutinous rubbish!'

Cherry held her breath, stifling a cry of dismay

caused by the disastrous attitude adopted by the girl whose emerging sexual awareness demanded the instant gratification of a hungry child. She had only secondhand knowledge of the havoc and agony felt by a youthful victim of unrequited love, yet her involvement had left her with a memory of heartbreak that would never fade. Her mind flew back in time to days spent humouring despairing moods, and nights spent trying to comfort her distraught sister Faith, then sixteen years old and three years younger than herself, who had fallen in love with the local Romeo and been thrown into an abyss of inconsolable misery by the news of his impending marriage.

'In that case,' Cherry winced in unison with Mistral, feeling old wounds re-opened by the cold, cutting edge of an authoritative male tongue, 'I suggest that, as you seem determined to sulk, you return to the beach and do so in private. By the time Cherry and I have finished lunch I shall expect to see some evidence of improvement in both manners and temper!'

Mistral glared and for tense, silent seconds seemed to be teetering on the verge of a rebellious tantrum. But suddenly, as if activated by a switch, she beamed Lucien a smile of audacious charm.

'Forgive me, *mon gardien*,' she cheeked him prettily. 'If I promise to be good will you allow me to stay?'

Stone would have melted beneath the warmth of her appeal, Cherry decided, feeling slightly dazed by Mistral's speedy transition from skittish foal to poised, well-behaved filly.

'And is our guest not also entitled to an

apology?' Though still curt, Lucien sounded distinctly mollified.

'*Certainement.*' Showing the quick contrition of a sinner eager to do penance, she turned soulful eyes upon Cherry. 'Please try to excuse my ill-mannered behaviour, *mademoiselle* ... or ...' her slight hesitation, her look of shy confusion set Cherry wondering if she had imagined Mistral's previous display of enmity. '... would you consider me forward if I were to ask to be allowed to call you Cherry?'

'Please do!' Cherry warmed to the overture of friendship from the girl whose fluctuating pattern of emotion was almost certainly a symptom of what her mother had been wont to refer to as the 'awkward age'.

Conveying gratitude with a gracious nod, Mistral sought to increase Lucien's approval by picking up her spoon to sample the thick, aromatic stew made of fish and shellfish, herbs and tomatoes which Cherry considered delicious.

'Hm, not bad,' she decided, slanting a look towards Lucien from beneath lowered lashes before turning to address Cherry in a conversational vein. 'I suppose I really should not turn up my nose at one of the traditional delicacies of our area. Familiarity breeds contempt, is that not so, Cherry? Have *you* ever been surprised by visitors to your country praising the taste of some simple meal that has appeared on your table with monotonous regularity for as long as you can remember? Or perhaps it is true that—according to a book I once read—the general attitude of your race towards food is that it should be plentiful and cheap rather than deliciously expensive and consequently available only to a fortunate few?'

'If put to the test, I dare say most of us would be prepared to accept a lower standard of sustenance in order that others might not go hungry,' Cherry smiled. 'But having said that, I must admit that I've often been surprised by demands from tourists, mostly well-fed Americans, for second helpings of drisheen, carrageen, and our world-famous stew.'

'Oh, yes . . .?'

When both Lucien and Mistral frowned with puzzlement, too well mannered to confess complete ignorance of the dishes she had mentioned, Cherry burst out laughing.

'Don't be afraid to admit that you've never heard of carrageen—a dish made from edible seaweed, or drisheen—a rather stodgy blood pudding, because if you were to travel the length and breadth of Ireland I doubt if you'd be served either in public eating places. We keep our pleasantest dishes concealed from the eyes of strangers and eat them solely within the privacy of our own homes!'

'Ireland . . .?' Lucien's quickened interest brought home to Cherry how foolishly she had allowed her tongue to ramble. 'But according to Diana both you and she are English?'

'She is . . . I am . . . we both are!' Carefully, Cherry laid down her spoon and clasped her hands tightly in her lap to control the trembling that never failed to erupt whenever she was forced with a need to explain her background and to answer the inevitable questions about her reasons for leaving home. Deciding to get the explanation over as quickly as possible, she began sketching a brief, stilted outline.

'My mother is Irish, but my father was an Englishman. Mother was barely eighteen when they met and married after a brief courtship. For almost a year they made their home in England, then, two months after I was born, my father was killed in a road accident. Naturally, my mother returned to her family home in Ireland. We lived with my grandparents for two years, until my mother remarried, this time to a neighbouring farmer, a childhood sweetheart, the man she had jilted in favour of my father.'

'And they have lived happily ever after, of course, and had lots more children?' Mistral prompted the proverbial happy ending.

'Lots more,' Cherry confirmed, outwardly bright, inwardly praying that she would be asked no further questions about her stepfather, Ryan, the coarse, bad-tempered Irishman who used his wife as a whipping post for vengeful pride, whose hatred of his stepdaughter had grown as strongly as her physical and characteristic likeness to the cultured, fair-haired, blue-eyed Englishman who had stolen his promised bride . . .

'How many more?' Mistral persisted.

'Six,' Cherry told her briefly, 'three girls and three boys.'

When Lucien leant forward to smile into her haunted blue eyes she felt the impact of his charm through her entire body.

'You surprise me, *ma chérie*—somehow or other I had not imagined you to be one of a large brood. The aura of serenity that wraps you like a cloak is more often indicative of a loveable and well-loved only child.'

Luckily, he appeared not to notice the start of
distress that might have led him to guess that she
had clothed naked hurt in a suit of armour, a
protective shell that had grown as she had grown
from a child bewildered by the actions of a
stepfather who had thrown curses her way instead
of kisses, to a girl who, because of constant
rejection, had been made to feel a social leper.

'There can be few people better qualified than
yourself to judge the merits and demerits of an
only child, Lucien,' Mistral broke in to tease. 'I
often wonder how you managed to survive a
childhood spent living in an island fortress with
only the company of servants to compensate for
the neglect of an absentee father. Mother has
always maintained that allowances should be made
for your moods of moroseness which she feels
certain are a consequence of an environment as
penalising as that of your mysterious ancestor!'

Cherry glanced curiously from Mistral's animated
face to Lucien's forbidding expression, intrigued by
this aspect of his character never previously
encountered. Moody ... Mysterious ... At that
moment, while she watched him brooding darkly
into a depth of dark red wine the adjectives seemed
justified. But quite plainly he was annoyed by
Mistral's choice of subject, so reluctantly, although
intensely interested, she decided not to pry.

However, Mistral, either because she was
oblivious to Lucien's displeasure or because she had
decided to ignore it in order to further the cause of
bright conversation, continued to enlighten Cherry.

'Are you familiar with the story of the "Masque
de Fer", Cherry?'

'Mask of Iron . . .?' Cherry interpreted, blankly shaking her head. Then her blue eyes brightened with a flash of inspiration. 'Oh, does it have any connection with a film that was made about some seventeenth-century nobleman who was imprisoned in a fortress and condemned to spend the rest of his days behind a mask of iron?'

'Voilà!' Mistral clapped with delight. 'Lucien, is it not gratifying to be part of a legend that has become familiar even to people living in isolated corners of the world?'

Lucien looked dour. 'I'm certain Cherry is too sensible to have been taken in by the sentimental claptrap portrayed by the movie screen,' he condemned, before lifting his glass and draining it dry.

Held fast by the grip of intense fascination, Cherry watched the sinuous rippling of neck muscles beneath tanned skin laid bare by the wide open collar of a black beach robe; a blade-sharp nose; clean-cut cheekbones and a sweep of jaw that could have been cast from iron. When he lowered his glass she looked away, ashamed of giving rein to such fanciful notions. Nevertheless, she was surprised and pleased when wryly Lucien picked up the threads of family history.

'My home, situated on an island in the Baie des Anges, did at one time have confined within its walls a former Duc de Marchiel whose face was reputed to have been kept screened by an iron mask until death put him out of his misery. But actually, it has been established that this person wore only a simple velvet mask. The riddle of his identity has never been positively established, some historians have claimed he was an illegitimate brother of Louis XIV, others say he was an accomplice of Madame la Brinvillieas, the poisoner. It has even been suggested by a recent researcher that a son born to the woman companion with whom the Man in the Iron Mask was provided was taken to Corsica, raised by unnamed foster-parents, and later became the great-grandfather of Napoleon.'

'*Entrusted* to foster-parents, Cherry!' Mistral stressed. 'Do you see the connection? Entrusted, translated into French, is '*remis de bon part*' and into Italian, '*di buona part*'—Buonaparte!' she concluded triumphantly.

'All mere conjecture, of course,' Lucien dismissed crisply. 'Even the name of the masked man was never revealed.'

'Except at his burial,' Mistral reminded quickly, when he was registered under the name of 'Monsieur de Marchiel'.

When Cherry, wide-eyed with wonder, expelled a breath of awe Mistral broke into a peal of laughter.

'Are you alarmed by the knowledge that you are in such exalted company, Cherry? Don't worry,' her mocking words could have been threaded with a soupçon of regret, 'the days are long gone when the House of Marchiel demanded of its prisoners instant obedience to the command written into its motto. *"Bon gré, mal gré"*,' she menaced softly. 'Willingly or unwillingly—whether one will or will not!'

Once lunch had been concluded with an iced chocolate mousse topped with whipped cream and flavoured with orange, Cherry felt able to take her leave without fear of giving offence. She had begun finding Mistral's overt remarks tiresome and Lucien's presence overpowering. Also, she was confused by the effect he had upon her senses, puzzled by the fact that in spite of having had his earlier frightening behaviour explained, her heart still leapt to attention at the sight of his rearing head, her hands still shook, her knees still trembled whenever he addressed her directly, and one glance from his keen eyes was sufficient to plunge her into a morass of shy uncertainty. Consequently, she was thrown into confusion when, after Mistral had wished her a polite *bonjour* and began sauntering slowly away, waiting for Lucien to catch her up, he slipped an arm around her shoulders and pleaded in a tone loud enough to reach the ears of his attentive ward:

'I refuse to wait until tomorrow to see you again! Please, *mon ange*, have dinner with me this evening?' As if sensing that her lips were rounding around a refusal, he insisted without giving her a chance to reply: 'I'll pick you up at your hotel about eight!'

The rejection trembling on her lips dissolved into an outraged gasp as she watched him striding out of sight with the confidence of a man born to rule, one inculcated from childhood with the assumption of power written into his arrogant family motto: *Bon gré, mal gré*—whether one will or will not!

Would she or would she not?

The question continued to tease her mind during hours spent—after slipping back to her hotel to change—pursuing her favourite pastime of a stroll around the flower, vegetable and fish markets that provided a boundless variety of colours, scents, and voluble, earthy characters.

First of all she made her way to the flower market. She never tired of gazing and sniffing at massed banks of flowers, every stall a cascading blossom-fall of tightly packed rosebuds each no bigger than a thumbnail, tied into fragrant bunches of pink, yellow, white, peach, cream and dark blood red, then plunged into tiered metal pails of cool water. The scent of carnations spiced the air; tall, slender lilies reminded her of weddings and shy, virginal brides; violets peeped; poppies flaunted; mimosa converged into fluffy yellow clouds around spiked honeysuckle, simple white marguerites, and prickly, oval plates of cacti.

By the time she had gazed her fill at market stalls brimming with baby courgettes, their golden blossoms still attached; deep purple aubergines; fresh green beans; long strings of garlic; mouth-watering mounds of strawberries; piles of shimmering sardines, anchovies, oursins, periwinkles, mussels, lobsters and scallops, she had relaxed into a state of satiated languor, so intoxicated with the smell, sight and colour of so many different foods she felt certain that the actual mechanics of eating would be beyond her.

But as she left the market-place behind and began wandering through the quaint narrow streets of the old town, towards the boutiques, cinemas, supermarkets, department stores and countless bistros cramming the modern shopping precinct situated to the rear of her hotel, euphoria gradually faded and problems temporarily shelved began surging to the forefront of her mind.

It had been unkind and very unfair of Diana to

attempt to burden her with responsibility for the welfare of innumerable unknown, unemployed and consequently impoverished members of the movie profession. Common sense told her that even the most hopeful and ambitious among them could not criticise her rejection of Lucien Tarascon's proposition, even though his promise to finance Marcus's next production was dependent upon her acceptance. Nevertheless, the seed of guilt sown by Diana had germinated and begun spreading roots of doubt in her fertile conscience. Then there was the threat to herself of being made homeless. Diana had proved herself ruthless, but never spiteful, yet the prospect of being turfed out, of having to search for somewhere to live in a large, unfriendly city, seemed a frightening possibility.

With such a daunting crisis looming mere days away, it seemed silly to be worrying mainly about Mistral. A girl enjoying every material advantage, but conversely one with whom she had discovered a strong affinity the moment she had seen her reduced to tears by the stinging lash of a man's insensitive tongue, seen her fawning like a puppy starved of affection, willing to accept a beating in exchange for a grateful lick ... Lucien Tarascon was a devil incarnate, she decided, pausing to gaze sightlessly into the interior of a bazaar that appeared to be stocked with nothing other than yards and yards of tee-shirts. He had no right to use wealth and privilege to manipulate people's actions to his own advantage, no right to demand two months of her life as the price of a contented conscience!

Her decision to stand firm, to refuse to be swayed by outside influences, had been firmly re-established by the time she entered the hotel and made her way up to the bedroom she shared with Diana. But the moment she stepped inside she was shocked to a standstill by the sight of doors flung wide disclosing an almost empty wardrobe, drawers pulled open, their contents left in piled-up disarray, and Diana bent across her bed stuffing small items of clothing down the sides of an almost filled suitcase.

'Diana, what on earth are you doing?' Cherry took a bewildered step forward, her wide eyes demanding even though her plummeting heart had already guessed the answer to her question.

'I'm preparing to fly to the States with Marcus!' Diana straightened defiantly. 'Nothing you can say will make me change my mind, Cherry, so please don't delay me by starting an argument, our plane's due to leave in an hour's time.'

Winded with amazement, Cherry sank down on her bed.

'But why? What guarantee of work will you have when you get there? What about your job—and there's the flat, you know I can't afford the rent if you're not there to share!'

'The lease has run out,' Diana informed her crisply. 'The landlord told me just before we left that if I intended to renew the rent would be doubled, so we'd have had to move out in any case. I'm sorry, Cherry, I would have told you sooner, but you're such a worrier I was afraid you might use the excuse of becoming homeless to cry off the holiday. But now everything's coming up roses!' she sparkled triumphantly, snapping shut the locks on her suitcase with a finality that

sounded to Cherry like the ramming home of a
bolt in a closed door of friendship.

Feeling swamped with hurt, she nevertheless had
to voice a worried suspicion.

'Marcus has made no secret of the fact that he's
prepared to go to almost any lengths in order to
fulfil the condition laid down by Lucien as part of
their agreement. Don't you *see*, Diana,' she
pleaded urgently, 'that by encouraging you to
leave me in the lurch Marcus could be attempting
to force my hand! When he discovers, as
eventually he must, that I've refused to give in to
combined pressure applied by himself, you and
Lucien Tarascon, he might leave you stranded in a
faraway country without money, with nowhere to
live and not a friend to turn to!'

As she paused to consider this possibility
Diana's flushed cheeks paled. Cherry saw doubt
and indecision chasing across her features, but
knew she had lost the argument when Diana's
shoulders lifted in a shrug of bravado. She braced
for the inevitable, then shrank from the look
almost of dislike projected by Diana's hard, raking
glance.

'You're trying to get me to change my mind on
your own account, not mine!' she accused
contemptuously. 'But it won't work, Cherry; such
a chance may never come my way again! And you
can cut out the reproachful looks, my conscience is
clear—I may be leaving you broke and very nearly
homeless, but you do have the option of earning
more in a couple of months than you normally do
in one year by taking up Lucien's offer! He thinks
you're an actress projecting a shy retiring image,
so why disabuse him?' she shrugged. 'Why not

fulfil his conditions by carrying on as normal, reacting to each given set of circumstances according to your conscience—he's never likely to suspect that a mask of open truth is covering up deception!'

Grabbing her suitcase, she strode towards the door, then almost on the threshold she hesitated to throw down a challenge.

'I'm prepared to gamble with chance and risk the consequences. The question is, Cherry, being such an honest, conscientious little prig, *are you*?'

For a long time after the door had slammed shut behind Diana, Cherry remained stretched out on her bed in a state of dazed apprehension, wondering how she could cope with the intricacies of airport procedure, and finally with the task of hunting through a maze of sleazy bedsitters in search of a suitable place to live. She lacked the assurance, the determination, the sheer brazen nerve that had enabled Diana to set off blindly as an astronaut towards an unknown planet, aware that the ground could fall away beneath her feet, yet willing to gamble all in a bid for stardom.

Finally, when she felt in danger of allowing fear to rob her mind of reasoning, she rolled off the bed and plodded across to the bathroom, unconsoled by the knowledge that for once she would be able to enjoy a good long soak without the aggravation of hearing Diana banging on the door urging her to hurry.

Some semblance of calmness had returned by the time she slipped a bathrobe over her still trembling limbs and twisted a towel turbanwise around hair fragrant with the wet-lavender perfume of her favourite shampoo. Desultorily, she began tidying up the mess that Diana had left in the bedroom, but the yawning space inside the wardrobe, drawers that looked capacious holding only her own meagre possessions, merely served to increase her sense of loss, to emphasise her loneliness to such an extent that a reminder of Lucien's invitation filled her with a sensation of relief. The very thought of eating caused her throat to tighten, but the company of anyone—even Lucien Tarascon—was preferable to an evening spent wrestling with chaotic thoughts.

A glance at her watch confirmed that she had less than half an hour in which to get ready. She whipped the towel from her head, then groped inside a drawer for a hairdryer. Fifteen minutes later, with her hair brushed smooth and twisted into a shimmering coil around her head, she surveyed the contents of her wardrobe wondering how she had managed to convince herself that a variety of versatile tee-shirts could supply outfits to be worn around the clock—even around the world!

With a resigned shrug she lifted a black, long-sleeved tee-shirt from a hanger and carefully eased its deeply vee-d neckline over her head. Then she teamed it with a silky black skirt, a gold belt, matching sandals, and a small gold envelope purse that she had picked up in the local flea market the previous day for just a few francs. There was just sufficient time left to apply a minimum of make-up—a brush of mascara across blonde lashes and brows, a smudge of deep violet eye-shadow, a trace of rose pink lipstick over a quivering mouth, and she was ready. With the hands of her watch indicating that she had mere seconds to spare, she draped a large silk-fringed shawl over her arm and without a backward glance sped out of the bedroom towards the stairs.

CHAPTER FIVE

NOT until she had actually begun descending the final flight of stairs leading down to the hotel foyer did Cherry recall the existence of a lift, or realise that Diana's absence had dispensed with the need to stage-manage a dramatic eye-catching entrance. So she was forced to proceed, her colour heightened by the conclusion of vanity sardonically emblazoned upon the lips of the man waiting at the foot of the stairway to greet her.

Yet there must have been something in her expression that moved him to kindness, or perhaps he was merely being mindful of a dependant's need for diplomacy when he greeted her with far less sarcasm than she had expected.

'*Bon soir, ma chérie!* As usual, you have achieved attention by dressing with riveting understatement! Is it talent or shrewdness that leads you to bait your hook with simplicity whenever you angle for praise?'

She stiffened with dislike of the man whose mouth always seemed to greet her appearance with a curl of amusement. Then, recalling her need of companionship, however satanic, she schooled her voice to respond pleasantly to his satire.

'Are you praising or criticising, *monsieur*?'

When he plucked the shawl from her arm to drape it around her shoulders her nerve ends reared to the stroke of fingers trespassing, apparently without intent, from the folds of the shawl on to a cool, silken slope of shoulder.

'I would not presume to review a book that I had not thoroughly studied,' he assured her in a low seductive undertone. 'As yet, I am familiar only with the title and the cover, both of which have succeeded in doing what they were specifically designed to do—please the eye, and excite interest in the contents of the first chapter.'

Something deep inside her responded with a quiver of apprehension to the man whose eyes she dared not meet, but whose features she knew were etched with the cynicism of an experienced philanderer who had lived too hard, loved too often and too unwisely.

'Let us go, *ma petite*,' he growled, complacent as a tiger anticipating a tasty titbit. 'We French believe that the din of hunger makes one deaf to reason; let us dine well so that, let us hope, we may reconcile our differences.'

Small wonder Mistral was attracted to him as a child is attracted to fire, Cherry thought, as nervously she allowed him to lead her outside the hotel to where a low-slung open-top sports car was parked close to the curb. His dominating air, the way he took the lead even in conversation, a sophisticated charm that was devastating whenever he chose to exercise it, were more than any near-schoolgirl, even one as precocious as Mistral, could possibly handle. But at least *she* was immune, she decided, as Lucien helped her into the front passenger seat before sliding behind the wheel. She had passed through the fire of one man's cruel treatment and like a mound of soft clay had come out hardened, made durable by a tough protective glaze. Obviously, Lucien Tarascon, wealthy socialite, jet-setting playboy whose photograph she had become accustomed to seeing in glossy magazines with always a bevy of young, beautiful girls in the background, was piqued by the novelty of having his wishes thwarted and was preparing to aim in her direction a barrage of the irresistible charm which in the past had helped him to get everything he had wanted.

Purely to test out her defences, she cast him a sideways glance as he sat alert behind the wheel waiting for a break in the stream of traffic. To protect his eyes from the glare of sunshine he had donned the sort of dark, wrap-around glasses favoured by celebrities who wished to remain unrecognised, but his dark silk suit, immaculate shirt, and discreetly patterned tie lent him the sombre air of a business man impatient to transact an important deal. Quickly, she turned her head aside, digging a biting reminder of a need for calm into a panicking bottom lip, bolstering her sagging optimism with the assurance that coolness would be an effective defence against the impatience she sensed simmering beneath his controlled movements, that whenever fire and water went to war, fire was the inevitable loser . . .

'As you have been confined to Cannes since your arrival, I thought you might enjoy a drive along the coast before we turn inland to dine at one of my favourite restaurants,' he began a pleasant opening salvo.

Fractionally, her guard slipped as she savoured the enticing prospect.

'That sounds blissful!' Ignoring his glance of amusement, Cherry relaxed with a sigh of pleasure into the seductive embrace of plump, suede-covered upholstery to drink in the sight of deep blue sea deepening to emerald where it fringed the shore; colourful sails floating lazily around Cap d'Antibes; the palm-lined sweep of promenade and a glimpse of off-shore islands veiled by a mist of heat.

'Sunshine helps you to forget your troubles, does it not, *ma chérie*?' Lucien's teeth flashed brilliant against his dark Riviera tan. 'It makes the cicadas sing, the waves dance, the sky grow blue and cloudless.'

'You're fortunate to be able to live where winter does not exist,' she told him shyly.

'Ah, but our climate is not entirely a mixture of eternal spring and Indian summer,' he teased as he edged the car out of the crowded Croisette and on to a gradually inclining road topped with houses rearing high against a skyline dominated by a background of distant mountains. 'Nothing is perfect. Just as peaches are prone to blight and cream has a tendency to curdle, the serpent in our Riviera paradise is first and foremost the *mistral*, a great wind which locals declare is sent by people from the north who are jealous of our fine weather. It has a curiously regular pattern of behaviour, blowing for a specific number of days that is always a multiple of three. As we drive farther into the mountains you will notice that the houses have all been built facing the same direction, pointing forward into the *mistral*, their northerly sides protected by hedges of cypress trees and their southern terraces shielded from the rays of summer sun by thickly foliaged plane trees.'

Unaware of the indulgent smile playing around

his lips, Cherry literally gaped as they drove past luxurious villas, places of refuge built along a stretch of coast made famous as one of the last retreats of the world's highly privileged. As if beautiful surroundings, endless sunshine and a glorious vista of deep blue sky and sea were not enough, Cherry condemned mutely, rich, pampered socialites had to import extra luxuries too!

Impervious to a simmering disapproval that had no relation to envy, Lucien tossed further fuel on to her impatience.

'Another day, when we have more time to spare, you must visit my apartment, which is not far from here. It is one of a block of buildings cleverly designed and constructed to represent the waves of the sea, the outer walls curved in such a manner that each patio garden has been rendered private and has an unobstructed view of the facing Baie des Anges.'

Cherry remained silent, feeling swamped by this insight into a lifestyle totally polarized from her own, dismayed by the unfairness of fate that had showered upon Lucien Tarascon an abundance of material possessions while deciding that she, in company with many thousands of others, should be reduced to the penury of being unable to afford the amount of money required to rent a modest bed-sitter.

Sunshine glittered upon chrome-decorated limousines parked upon drives kept meticulously shaven by an army of gardeners. Swimming pools flashed turquoise and blue between gaps in hedges of purple bougainvillaea. Yachts and speedboats bobbed at anchor next to landing stages jutting from small private beaches. And above the roof of one particularly imposing residence a helicopter hovered over a landing pad tucked into an unobtrusive corner of its extensive grounds. High above the noisy, traffic-jammed Croisette the air hung still and silent, reeking with the aroma of wealth and its accompanying essences of privilege and power.

Then suddenly the road dipped and pink-washed villas gave way to sturdy-looking houses built of grey stone. Cherry's deflated spirits soared when the road plunged downward into a tree-lined gorge, its towering sides scattered with limestone rocks, pierced with caves, shrouded in absolute silence. Lucien left her to savour the scene in peace as he concentrated all his attention upon negotiating a narrow road twisted into hairpin bends and blind corners, one moment dipping towards the bed of a crystal-clear river, the next racing up past delightful little villages nestling among orange groves and vineyards, where old men sat in the shade of gnarled old olive trees; where bouquets of white broom tempered the blaze of purple bougainvillaea clinging to roadside walls.

'What a contrast to the scenery along the coastline!' she gasped when they emerged from a dark tunnel of trees into a mist of spray rising from water flung like a narrow bolt of silver satin from the rim of the gorge to plunge, frothing and creaming, into the river running beneath a bridge just wide enough to accommodate their car.

'As complex as the character of the true Provençal,' Lucien agreed, disappointing her by driving straight on. 'A man of Provence has been described as being sociable yet selective, welcoming only those whom he considers to be his equals yet, conversely, renowned for his friendly attitude towards tourists. Even so, he is careful to ensure that there is no access to his gardens from the street! He likes the good things of life, yet seriousness and gravity are always near the surface; he can be sensitive, imaginative, sympathetic and amusing, yet he is cautious and slow to reach a decision.

'However,' he tossed her an engaging grin, 'there is also a second school of thought that brands him as wild and brutal as his mountain environment. Tell me, *ma chérie*,' he asked her almost idly, 'what do you think of the theory that suggests a man's character is moulded by the environment in which he has been raised?'

Gravely, she considered his question, her thoughts winging back to the house her mother had tried to make into a home; to her subdued, obedient sisters, and the stepbrothers who had grown into exact replicas of their uncouth, insensitive father.

'I think it must hold some element of truth,' she decided, the bleak tone of her voice giving away more than she knew. 'People are like plants, the goodness of their yield is dependent upon the sort of nourishment they receive and also upon the situation of the soil into which the seeds have been sown.'

He could not possibly have read her mind, yet his question seemed too apt to be merely coincidental.

'How often do you visit your family, *ma chérie*?'

'Just once a year—at Christmastime,' she admitted briefly.

'Ah, *calenda me li sieu*! "Spend Christmas with your folks," ' he translated softly, 'an old saying which my servants are fond of quoting in my hearing whenever the festival draws near.'

Adroitly, because she suspected he might revert to probing further, Cherry switched the subject of their conversation away from her own affairs.

'If your servants are permitted to join their families at Christmas, then where do you go?'

Keeping his eyes trained upon the winding road, he lifted his shoulders in a very Gallic shrug of indifference.

'Usually I go skiing.'

'Alone?' She had not meant to sound so incredulous, and wished the word unsaid when one wickedly tilted eyebrow reminded her of tales told by Diana about his many sexual adventures—tales whose truth seemed confirmed by his wicked growl of amusement.

'No,' he shook his head, 'I never go alone. Most of the year I congratulate myself upon the absence of family ties that are apt to grow irksome—but never at Christmastime, for it is then that solitude is most likely to adopt an ambience of solitary confinement.'

Cherry stared, surprised by the admission that a man who appeared to possess everything in the world he could possibly want, an Adam who had eaten every apple at least once, should be on probation, living with the ever-looming threat of imprisonment within a cell of loneliness.

Without stopping to think, she blurted:

'As you so obviously enjoy the company of women, I'm surprised that you've never married.'

'It is because I like the company of women, *many* women, that I have been careful to avoid the trap of matrimony,' he told her laconically.

She was relieved when the negotiating of a series of hairpin bends forced him to keep his attention on the road while he continued:

'I regard marriage as captivity, an end to freedom, an unnatural state within which a man is expected to confine his lovemaking to his chosen mate until death do them part. Falling in love is a pleasure that I am reluctant to deny myself, even though duty demands that someday I must conform to the custom of self-inflicted misery if only for the strictly practical purpose of providing an heir to inherit land and property that has been in my family's possession for centuries.'

Cherry felt a surge of outrage mixed with pity for the unfortunate girl destined to be tricked into marriage by a man whose sole aim was the procreation of his callous species, who would entice her towards the altar by pretending that she was loved and then afterwards have no compunction whatsoever about flouting the rules of fidelity.

'And no doubt,' her attempt to sound scoffing was spoiled by a wobble of indignation, 'you live by the double standard of morality which bestows upon you a right to indulge in extra-marital affairs yet justifies the expectation of total fidelity from your unfortunate wife!'

'Certainly,' he agreed with a matter-of-fact coolness that prodded her gentle nature into an incensed furor. 'But I would not be so hypocritical as to take any woman in marriage without first making my conditions plain. I consider a life of luxury and a position in society a fair exchange for forbearance and for the honour of bearing my children—an occupation which, when all is said and done, is the be-all and end-all of female existence.'

Cherry had learnt from bitter experience that all men were selfish, immoral rogues, nevertheless, his iniquitous assumption left her shaken.

'You really believed it possible to find a woman willing to enter into such an arrangement?' she charged, incensed.

'I do,' he confirmed, his voice echoing the same casual ease with which he swung the bonnet of the car around a particularly awkward bend. 'I anticipate that the greatest drawback will be the difficulty of deciding which eventual young, healthy candidate for motherhood will be likely to prove the most fruitful.'

Mutely, Cherry sank back into her seat, defeated by the enormity of his conceit. In almost any other company the drive through the dramatic gorge misted with vapour from dozens of small waterfalls, up winding mountain roads, past villages scented with roses, melodic with the tinkling of cowbells, past fields of gently swaying lavender painted purple by the brush of twilight, would have been a delightfully tranquil experience. But as it was, the arrogant Duc had turned the outing into a test of endurance, a mistake she could hardly wait to rectify.

The first lights of evening had just begun twinkling from the windows of scattered farmhouses when Lucien drove between the gates of a garden dense with pines, laurel trees, grapevines and beds of carefully tended flowers. Ancient stones bearing inscriptions in Greek and Latin leant drunkenly along a drive leading to cloisters with rounded archways and eventually to a square courtyard where Lucien braked the car to a standstill.

'Originally, this place was built as a monastery.' His wave encompassed a stone building towering above the cloisters, its walls pitted with deep embrasures just wide enough to admit a slit of light into narrow, monastic cells, and the bell tower and steeple of a structure that had obviously been designed as a place of worship.

'Raids by Saracens and Genoese pirates, attacks by the Spaniards, and the consequent arrival of military garrisons, were not conducive to a peaceful, silent existence, so the monks moved out and eventually the monastery was sold,' he explained, cupping a hand beneath her elbow to guide her through tile-paved cloisters giving access to a garden where numerous paths were arrowed in the direction of a large vine-covered terrace.

'For many, many years it stood empty, until the almost derelict buildings were bought by an actress, a fugitive from the hell-broth of Paris, and it was she who, after living a twenty-year-long country idyll, founded the very excellent restaurant, Retreat, that continues to insist, even in this mercenary era, upon retaining a closely-vetted, highly-exclusive clientèle.'

Nervously, certain that she would be bound to fail to measure up to standards set by guardians of such unique, almost secretive privilege, Cherry peered into the dusk-shrouded garden laden with the incense of herbs, cyclamen and grape hyacinths, wondering if her tightly knotted stomach muscles would allow her to do justice to the sort of epicurean feast that had doubtless been prepared for a clientèle of blasé, over-indulged gourmets.

But much to her surprise the restaurant, when they eventually reached it, was a model of spartan simplicity. A scattering of rustic chairs and tables laid with plain white tablecloths were bathed in moonbeams filtering through gaps left in a ceiling of vine-covered trellis. Light from solitary candles set in the centre of individual tables cast just sufficient light to allow for comfortable vision yet blurred the features of seated patrons to indistinguishable profiles, one moment masked in shadow, the next made incandescent when bowed heads penetrated the flame-flicked nimbus of light cast by one low, crimson candle.

Gravel crunched under the thin soles of her evening slippers as Lucien urged her towards the fringe of the dining area to take occupation, as if by divine right, of a table set secluded as an eyrie perched high on a mountain top, with only a curved arm of balcony separating them from a plunge of velvet darkness sprayed with diamond droplets cast by a serried chain of floodlit waterfalls. The sound of water crashing on to rocks far below was audible yet muted enough to allow Lucien the pleasure of hearing the awed catch in her voice when she whispered:

'Oh, how sublimely beautiful! How exquisitely picturesque . . .!'

'As overwhelming as ecstasy, yet as simple as hunger,' he softly agreed. 'Sit down, *ma chérie*, drink in the spectacle in silence, for there really are no words available to do it justice.'

If the location, the atmosphere, and the scenery had been manufactured specifically to his own design they could not have induced within Cherry a more bemused, bewitched, blissful state of mind.

Somewhere deep in her subconscious she was
aware that her emotions were being deliberately
manipulated, charmed by an experienced seducer
whose mask of velvet hid a profile as cold and
heartless as iron, but an ambrosial liquor served in
thimble-sized glasses dripped honeyed balm upon
her fears, just as the solicitious charm, the care he
expended upon consulting her wishes so that she
was served exactly the kind of food she preferred,
introduced her to the strange new joy of feeling
cossetted, an experience that caused her vision to
become dazzled by stars dancing with excitement
in her deep blue eyes. While she was eating a rich,
delicious fish soup and Lucien was initiating her
into the local custom of spreading croutons with
herb-flavoured mayonnaise before dipping each
one into a dish of grated cheese, small brown
birds—the first she had seen since her arrival in
Cannes—hopped between the tables in search of
crumbs, and background water music played
continuously, on and on, throughout courses
created by an eminent *cuisinier* for his *corps d'élite*.
Delectable foie gras garnished with peeled and
pipped grapes, tender gigot of lamb with crisply
cooked vegetables, cheese for Lucien and for
herself a caramel-flavoured charlotte piped with
whipped cream and decorated with pieces of
marrons glacés.

Then as a final delight, just as coffee was being
poured into tiny eggshell china cups, a waiter
approached carrying a tray bearing a present.

'Just a small *bonne-bouche* for the lady,' he
bowed to Cherry, 'with the compliments of the
proprietor.'

'*Merci*, Pierre.' Smoothly, Lucien expressed into

words her gasp of pleasure. 'Please convey to the chef our appreciation of a splendid meal, and also our thanks to the proprietor, Monsieur Dauphine.'

Cherry heard the crackle of a note changing hands before the waiter faded into obscurity, leaving them to enjoy once more an illusion of solitude, of being set apart in a universe consisting of moonlight, star-spangled sky and the soporific incense of night scented blossoms.

Dreamily, she poked a finger inside a dainty beribboned basket filled with delectable sweet imitations of silver-foiled sardines, mussels, oysters, snails, finely grained pebbles, nuts, berries, and truffles rolled in dark cocoa to achieve exactly the matt surface of real truffles she had seen displayed in the market place.

'Does Monsieur Dauphine present all his lady guests with the same charming keepsake?' she asked Lucien, unaware that his lips were twitching with amusement as he watched her transferring a smudge of cocoa from a finger on to a childishly pink tongue.

'Each lady is accorded an attribute to whichever virtue she happens to be parading,' he confirmed cynically. 'Henri Dauphine prides himself upon being an expert judge of character. Immediately, at first sight—or so he claims—he is able to partner a woman with one of his stock of complimentary gifts. One single red rose for the dark sophisticate; a tiny phial of lavender perfume for the not so very young; for the sexy blonde a naughty black lace garter, and for the sweet innocent——' he broke off to glance at the basket of sweets she had lovingly cupped between her palms, then suddenly dissolved into laughter. 'I'm sorry, *mon ange*,' he responded to her look of puzzlement by struggling to regain his composure, 'my laughter was not meant unkindly—on the contrary, it is more of a tribute to your skill as an actress, because for the first time ever Henri Dauphine has been fooled!'

Somehow or other, in spite of the fact that her pleasure in the gift had been completely demolished, Cherry managed to suppress an indignant retort. But not the frown which he was quick to notice.

'Is something troubling you, *ma chérie*? I would not want anything to spoil this delightful evening.'

But for her the evening was already spoiled—as tattered as a fragile web torn by a harsh wind of reality. Problems flooded back to the forefront of her mind, drowning every star in her eyes, leaving them bleak, dark, and intensely troubled.

'Marcus has persuaded Diana to accompany him to America. I'm terribly concerned about her . . .'

'You are?' Careless eyebrows winged. 'But why, you are both women of the world, are you not? Actresses are purported to abide by a different code of conduct from most of their sex. Being less inhibited, members of your profession are consequently more likely than most to follow the finger of opportunity whenever and wherever it may beckon.'

He had not actually sneered, but his derogatory tone caused her to flare. 'If you think me so lacking in propriety, why didn't you approach me directly with an invitation to dine instead of cooking up an elaborate plot with Marcus?'

'Because to have responded with alacrity to one who had not been properly introduced would not have been consistent with your image,' he declared with such calculated cruelty she gasped. 'Every year during Film Festival week Cannes is thronged with ambitious actresses, their minds determinedly set upon the type of role they wish to portray—the *bête noire*; the *femme fatale*; some who are intensely earthy, others dramatically drab. During latter years your type has become more and more rare—as you have probably cleverly deduced—but unfortunately only a person of your talent is capable of projecting a convincing image of the sort of girl my cousin wishes her daughter to become. Although I have tried to explain to her that the sweet *ingénue* disappeared from the scene some twenty years ago and that virtue, modesty, and all similiar feminine attributes have been banished to the realms of mythology, she refused to listen and persists in her demand that Mistral should be protected from all modern permissive influences. Naturally,' he shrugged, 'that is utterly impossible. Nevertheless, duty has compelled me to seek out a passable imitation of the extinct female paragon so that Mistral might miraculously benefit from her example during the last remaining weeks of my guardianship.

'But also, *ma chérie* . . .' When he hesitated, Cherry wondered for a moment whether a trick had been played upon her imagination by a passing breeze teasing the candle flame and casting a shadow across his features that could almost have been mistaken for embarrassment.

'. . . only *le bon Dieu* knows why,' he continued awkwardly, 'but Mistral's moods and emotions are threatening to become unmanageable. I do not wish to deal ruthlessly with her infatuation, yet I dare not be kind. Which is why I have decided to make my proposition more inviting—I am in urgent need of your co-operation, *petite*!'

She experienced a shocking sense of power when his fingers dug a plea for compassion into the soft flesh of her arm.

'You may lay down your own conditions, name your own price, if only you will help me to cure Mistral of her obsession by pretending for two months only to be my radiant fiancée—one who fell in love almost at first meeting and was swept into a betrothal without being given a chance to change her mind!'

CHAPTER SIX

CHERRY cast one last look around her hotel bedroom before reaching for the telephone to request the help of a porter to transfer her luggage downstairs.

Regrets were useless, she decided, and in any case it was now too late to change her mind. Letters had been written and despatched, one to her boss quoting the feeble 'circumstances beyond my control' excuse for her prolonged absence; the other a pleading letter to Diana's landlord asking that the lease of the flat be transferred to her name and enclosing a cheque for two months' rent in advance.

Lucien had provided her with the money, and that, of course, was another reason why she could not back out of the deceitful charade. Half of the very generous sum he had offered in exchange for her co-operation was already deposited in her bank account, the rest to be paid in two months' time when Mistral's vacation was over and she would be returning to spend her last full term at finishing school.

Lucien had also made a very efficient job of tying up various other loose ends—Cherry's flight had been cancelled, the tour operator and other officials had been informed of her extended visit, and in a few minutes' time she was due to vacate her hotel bedroom.

In a scared, almost hypnotised trance, she

forced rigid limbs to transport her outside on to the balcony where she stood staring out across the bay trying to penetrate the heat haze behind which lay the tiny island which for the next couple of months was to be her home.

What on earth had possessed her to fall in with Lucien Tarascon's wishes?

Whether concern for Diana's welfare had been paramount, or intense pity for Mistral whose tender young feelings she had agreed must be hurt for the sake of her own good; whether it had been that the amount of the bribe Lucien had offered was sufficient to rid her completely of the threat of destitution, or simply that she had been foolish enough to allow her senses to be bewitched by magical surroundings, delectable food, and the persuasive tongue of a professional charmer made little difference now that promises had been exchanged. She had sold two months of her life to the devil, had agreed to pretend affection for a man within whose character was encapsulated all the vices and vagaries of Dante's assortment of devils—Alichino, the allurer; Barbariccia, the malicious; Calcobrian, the grace scorner; Dragnignazzo, the fell dragon; Libicocco, the ill-tempered; Rubicante, the red with rage; Scarmiglione, the baneful; Caynazzo, the snarler; Ciriato Sannuto, the tusked boar . . .!

When the telephone shrilled a summons across the silent bedroom she jerked violently with fright, then hurried to pluck the receiver into trembling fingers.

'*Bonjour, mademoiselle,*' a polite voice responded to her prompting, 'Monsieur le Duc de Marchiel sends his compliments. He has just arrived and says that he will wait in the foyer until you are ready to join him.'

'Tell him . . . tell him I'm ready now,' she drew in a long steadying breath, 'and that I won't keep him waiting more than a couple of minutes.'

She waited until a porter had departed with her luggage before crossing to a mirror to cast a frowning look at her reflection. Unlike Diana, she had not been able to afford a special wardrobe of beachwear to be worn exclusively during the three precious holiday weeks which were all she was allowed each year. Every garment in her wardrobe had been planned to lead a double life—a silk pyjama top had to do duty as a blouse; culottes had to be pulled over a swimsuit doubling as a bandeau top. Lucien Tarascon had betrayed a keen eye for fashion and though she felt certain he would not disapprove of tanned legs, pretty pastel pumps, sleeveless cotton sweater and a plaited leather belt, she wondered if he was astute enough to realize that her frilled silk skirt had originally been designed to be worn as a petticoat.

'Ah, well,' she sighed, cramming a straw panama on the back of her head, 'at least I did invest in one up-to-the-minute accessory!'

Being mindful to make use of the lift, she was swooshed silently down to the ground floor and disgorged at the rear of the foyer where she was able to linger for a few minutes unobserved to scan the faces of milling occupants. Almost immediately she spotted Lucien sitting in an armchair, looking perfectly relaxed, his well groomed head bent over a newspaper, his long legs stretched out, comfortably crossed at the ankles. Her heart lurched, dismayed by the discovery that his attire was far less casual than her own, his choice of fawn lightweight suit, cream silk shirt and dark brown, unpatterned tie seemingly indicative of an intention to follow some form of pursuit that she had not anticipated.

She turned on her heel, half panicked into flight, then was halted by a reminder that there was no place left to which she could run! She was still wavering, flushed with indecision, when Lucien's eyes lifted from his newspaper and swung towards her. At once he rose to his feet and strode across the foyer to greet her.

'*Bonjour, ma belle fiancée!*' His dancing eyes, humorous mouth and teasing form of address seemed to signify that she was in for a day of torment.

'Good morning,' she responded, unable to force stiff lips to smile. 'I appear to be inappropriately dressed.' She cast a deprecating look at her outfit. 'If only you'd informed me of your plans I could have——'

'For the moment dress is unimportant,' he breezed, giving an impression of being well pleased with himself and with life in general. 'I do realise that your wardrobe has been planned to act as a foil for your image of sweet simplicity. However, circumstances have changed. As you are now my fiancée and the supposed future Duchesse de Marchiel, it will no longer be considered *comme il faut* for you to be seen walking the streets in your underwear. That is why,' his wide grin mocked her embarrassed rise of colour, 'the next few hours are to be spent shopping!'

In spite of her tongue-tied resentment, the threat of having to delve into her precious store of money in order to meet the extortionate prices marked up by owners of Riviera boutiques forced passed her lips a sharp protest.

'But I can't afford——'

'Don't worry,' he eyed her with cool cynicism, 'you will not be expected to rob your own coffers. Whatever we may purchase may be regarded as a bonus—a perk—a word which has, I believe, been coined especially by the English to describe the dishonest rite of extracting more from a contract than was originally agreed. Before our amorous experiment gets under way, *ma chérie*,' the thread of menace running through his words was made all the more riveting by a thin, unwavering smile, 'let it be clearly understood that, while you are welcome to retain any material benefits accruing from our association, the title of fiancée is merely out on loan!

'And now let's go!' He slid an arm around her waist and as if no electrifying insult had been flung her way, began directing her outside and on to the pavement of the busy Croisette.

'First we must purchase a ring to set a seal of authenticity upon our betrothal. Which stone do you prefer, *ma chérie*, emeralds, sapphires, or diamonds?'

She wanted to pull away, to stamp her feet, to rant and rave at the conceited, egotistical Duc who had just dared to warn her off falling in love with him! But the shock of learning that he could even consider such an event likely had left her so stunned that her blue eyes remained dazed even when he drew her to a standstill while he assessed the contents of a jeweller's window—a branch of a world-renowned firm whose shop stood adjacent to the hotel.

'Diamonds signify innocence, emeralds success in love. As neither stone seems appropriate,' he mused, 'perhaps we should consider sapphires after all.'

'An excellent choice!' The voice Cherry thought she had lost for ever returned with a snap. 'Considering it was employed by some ancients as an antidote to madness!'

'Then a sapphire it shall be,' he decided promptly. 'It will serve to remind both of us of the threat of insanity which, when all is said and done, is no more than a dream that has been allowed to run amok.'

But Cherry took fright immediately she stepped inside the interior of a shop that was different from any she had previously entered. The sort of jewellers she frequented usually had a treasure trove of wares displayed from floor to ceiling, assistants bustling behind showcase counters crammed with watches, rings, pendants and trinkets of all descriptions. They did not have floors cushioned with soft, dove grey carpet; elegant chairs set around circular, highly polished occasional tables; one solitary presence whose attire was formal and whose attitude looked forbidding; and—except for a few ornaments placed as unobtrusively as items around an everyday living-room—a total absence of goods for sale.

Mentally condemning the self-absorption that had caused her to overlook signals of gilt-edged superiority no doubt being emitted from a similarly discreet window display, she grabbed the sleeve of Lucien's jacket and tugged him to a standstill.

'Let's get out of here!' she hissed. 'It looks far too expensive . . .'

For a second he looked taken aback, then decidedly pained.

'*Mon Dieu!*' he clamped while still out of earshot of the approaching salesman. 'I can understand an actress's need to "get inside the skin of a part", but must you continue to perform even when I am your only audience?'

'*Bonjour, mademoiselle—Monsieur Marchiel.*' Even as the sales assistant was bowing politely to Cherry his eyes were pivoting towards Lucien. 'Can I be of any assistance?'

'You certainly can,' Lucien nodded easily. 'We would like to see a collection of rings—my fiancée has decided that she has a preference for sapphires.'

The sales assistant did not allow so much as a flicker of eyelashes to register surprise, yet instinctively Cherry sensed that Lucien was a frequent and valued customer and that she had been sized up and judged the latest of a long line of *petites amies*.

With hot colour racing into her cheeks, she sank into one of the two chairs the assistant hastened to draw up to a convenient table and tried to appear unconcerned while he draped a black velvet cloth over its surface before murmuring a request to be excused while he retreated to the strongroom to fetch a selection of appropriate items. The moment he moved out of earshot she rounded fiercely upon Lucien.

'I feel like a rich man's paramour, a cheap gold-digger! Why go to the expense of buying genuine stones when circumstances warrant no more than a satisfactory imitation?'

'Because members of the society in which you are shortly about to move can tell skimmed milk from cream at thirty paces,' he rebuked coldly. 'Paste jewels, unlike actresses, seldom manage a convincing display of qualities which they do not possess. Also . . .' she was left floundering when he directed a sudden, devastating smile, 'today I am feeling pleasantly inclined towards indulgence. In exchange for your agreeing to help me out of my difficulties, I wish to reward you with a trinket that might add a touch of glitter to your grey little soul.'

His audacious eyes dared her to argue when the assistant returned carrying several velvet-lined trays which he set down nearby before beginning, with the flourish of a magician producing surprises out of a hat, to set out individual items for inspection.

'Sapphires and diamonds mounted in platinum?' Reverently he placed upon the velvet cloth a ring made up of five square-cut sapphires sandwiched between two rows of glittering diamonds.

'No.' Lucien waved it aside, giving Cherry no time to comment. 'The stones are far too small.'

With eyes flashing bright as the gems he was handling the assistant laid the first and second trays aside, then delved into the third, his aloof composure threatened by a thin-lipped smile of satisfaction. The magnificence of the rings he produced took Cherry's breath away: a sapphire and diamond cluster: an oval solitaire with a collar of tiny pearls; a circular stone with built up shoulders of diamonds; gems shaped into flowers with glistening dark blue petals and diamond-bright leaves; then a glorious square-cut stone set like a patch of heaven inside a pearly cloud.

But to her utter amazement Lucien waved them all away, obviously still not satisfied.

'You disappoint me,' he frowned. 'Are you certain that these are the best you can offer?'

When Cherry's sharp ears caught the catch of an indrawn breath as the assistant lifted the last remaining tray from the adjacent table she sensed that he was about to produce his *pièce de résistance*.

'We do have this exceptionally fine sapphire ring, *monsieur*,' he leant to place the tray on the table in front of them, 'but unfortunately it is part of a suite and as such cannot be sold separately.'

Cherry stared, her eyes darkening to the same almost deep purple depth of the collection of jewels that had been set into a necklace resembling a chain of butterflies in flight, each with four oval-shaped sapphire wings attached to a tiny diamond-studded body. Two separate butterflies, one to alight upon each ear, and a small swarm meant to be clasped around the wrist were displayed artistically around one single jewelled ring bearing a similarly fashioned butterfly but with a larger body and wings.

'Ah, at last we are seeing a collection that truly merits the term "superb",' Lucien stated with a look of approval that sent Cherry's anxiety soaring into a state of agitation. 'Try this for size, *ma chérie*.' Lucien plucked the ring out of its bed of snow white velvet and slid it past a neatly trimmed, unvarnished nail until the exotic wings quivered to rest against her pale slim finger.

'I was beginning to suspect that we would have

to shop elsewhere,' he told the anxious sales assistant, 'that for once your establishment was not capable of supplying me with a gift complementary to the image of my companion. However, the butterfly motif captures exactly the fluttering, indecisive nature of my fiancée.'

'Like to like,' he murmured, cupping one nerveless hand in his palm, 'light, flippant, shallow young creatures that dart from pleasure to pleasure, demonstrating good humour when all is bright and when every prospect pleases, but becoming conspicuously absent when clouds begin to gather. Tell me,' he leant across the table to reach for her other hand,' could you bear to be parted from the pretty bauble nestling contented as a moth against your candle-pale finger?'

Cherry stared dazedly at her hand lying pale as cream against a palm tanned to the rich dark shade of coffee. He could not possibly be flirting with the notion of buying the whole suite of fabulously expensive-looking jewellery, she assured herself. And yet the sales assistant had quite definitely insisted that the ring was not to be sold separately! Deciding to err on the side of caution—because she had learnt to her cost that resistance acted like a spur upon his determination—she did not argue, but attempted to respond humorously to his observation.

'The ring is certainly superb,' she nodded, 'but I would prefer not to have a permanent reminder of having once been likened to a creature that is notably self-destructive.'

'Because you cannot see yourself ever being weak enough, nor even sufficiently attracted by temptation to allow your wings to become scorched?' he taunted.

'No,' she managed a whisper that she hoped the hovering assistant would find inaudible, 'because the scorch marks of rejection take a very long time to heal.'

Suddenly his smile faded. 'Experience should be regarded as wisdom acquired rather than as illusions lost,' he chided with an irritated shrug. 'Simply because some man once left you in the lurch you should not make hurt your excuse for being afraid of living.'

Looking far more annoyed than Cherry had given him cause to be, he rose to his feet and uttered a curt instruction to the sales assistant.

'The sapphires will do nicely. Mademoiselle will continue to wear the ring—have the rest of the items packaged ready to be collected later!'

After leaving the shop Cherry was surprised by the discovery that Lucien appeared to be in no hurry to retreat from Cannes. In spite of oppressive heat and the restrictive formality of his attire, for the following couple of hours he shepherded her around the most exclusive shops, encouraging her to try on wickedly expensive shoes; to sniff scent costing thousands of francs for a two-ounce bottle; to admire crocodile skin handbags and Hermès silk scarves, and even insisted—much to her heated astonishment—upon her slipping her arms into the sleeves of a long, glossy brown Russian sable coat.

As reluctantly she pandered to his whim, feeling inferior as a rabbit draped in ostentatious pelts, a bright flash of light exploded in front of her eyes, shocking her face white and blinding her completely.

'What was that? What happened . . .?' She

blinked rapidly, trying to focus shocked eyes upon Lucien.

'You are surely familiar with the effects of a flashbulb?' When her vision cleared she saw that he was smiling broadly. 'It was nothing—probably a shop assistant fooling around with a camera. I'm tired of shopping,' he decided irritably, 'let's look for a place to have lunch.'

Suppressing an impulse to remind him that the occupation had been one of his own choosing, Cherry simmered in silence while he guided her outside on to the pavement, then turned left, obviously heading for one of the plush hotel restaurants looking over the noisy, fume-laden Croisette.

'Lucien . . .!' She halted determinedly, metaphorically digging in her heels. 'Must we have lunch in a hotel—I'd much rather eat in a bistro?'

When his eyebrows drew together she thought he was about to refuse, but then unexpectedly his mouth relaxed into a smile of capitulation.

'Very well, Charity Sweet, if it will please you,' he teased, cupping a hand beneath her elbow to urge her suddenly leaden limbs forward. 'There is a bistro not far from here, a typical tourist trap with chequered tablecloths, candles guttering in the necks of empty wine bottles, and a waiter wearing a striped vest and jaunty beret who plays "La Vie en Rose" over and over again on his accordion. But I must warn you that the food will probably be cold and the wine execrable!'

The place was everything he had claimed, even down to the music which at any other time Cherry would have found heart-stirring. But she barely heard the melody because of the agitated drumming in her ears, tasted neither food or drink while she nerved herself to discover which other secrets he had managed to unearth.

'How ... how did you find out that my name is Charity?' she finally managed to croak.

'By looking inside your passport. You asked me to collect it, along with the rest of your valuables, from the concierge's office, if you remember.'

The simple explanation came as such an anticlimax that for seconds she just stared mutely with every vestige of serenity drained from her face.

'Why the fuss? Do you object to me calling you Charity?'

'Yes!' Baldly, she ejected the statement through teeth clenched to prevent them from chattering.

'Ah!' His eyes narrowed keenly. 'Because that name is sacred to the man who hurt you so much, is that not so?'

'Yes!' Hurt was forcing her to make her responses monosyllabic, painful memories of the man who had never allowed her the privilege of calling him father, but had always insisted that she should address him as infrequently as possible and only when forced to resort to using his christian name.

As if annoyed by her absorption in thoughts, Lucien prompted curtly:

'What is the name of this ghost that haunts you?'

'Ryan ...' She bit out the name as if it had scalded her tongue.

'Then Ryan has my sympathy,' he decided cruelly, 'for he has probably discovered that far from being free, Charity can develop into an extremely costly virtue!'

CHAPTER SEVEN

CHERRY'S outfit had been chosen with a boat trip in mind. She had imagined that Lucien would be eager to transfer herself and her luggage to his island home immediately she vacated the hotel, consequently, when they left the bistro she settled in the passenger seat of his car expecting to be driven towards the Gare Maritime, from which ferryboats departed frequently carrying passengers and freight to a scattering of tiny offshore islands.

But without a word of explanation he set off along the Boulevard de la Croisette, passed the Palm Beach and a breathtaking view of Golf-Juan Bay, then continued along by the shore until they reached a branch in the road signposted Antibes.

Wondering if she dared enquire the reason behind the choice of direction, she chanced a sideways glance and was immediately deterred by the sight of a scowl casting a depth of displeasure over a profile as forbidding as the Masque de Fer that was purported to have been clamped around the features of a previous Duc de Marchiel.

She turned aside to gaze out of the car window, determined to enjoy as much as she was able of her brief incursion into high society, to store up memories that might help to relieve a little of the loneliness she would be bound to feel once she returned home to an empty flat.

The road inclined higher and higher, curving

like a protective arm around a magnificent bay, its gently sloping beach of fine sand protected from the wind by the sumptuous Cap d'Antibes. She craned forward in her seat, envying the privacy and solitude afforded to occupants of villas perched high on granite cliffs with smooth steps cut into their jagged surface providing easy access to sickles of private beach. Then her breath caught in a gasp of pure delight when she glimpsed a pine wood flowing green as a cataract over the rim of a cliff straight down to the sea. Adjacent was a large building built in the form of serried arcs opening on to a magnificent vista of sky and sea, its grey cement walls harmonising so well with its surroundings that the structure appeared to merge into its rocky background.

Then, in spite of sunshine crisping around the crown of her straw boater, she shivered, feeling a chill of premonition that seemed justified when seconds later Lucien ran the car off the road and steered it through the creeper-framed entrance of a tunnel that sloped gradually down into an underground car park which, except for themselves, was entirely empty.

'Come, let me show you my apartment!'

Lucien slid from his seat and walked around the bonnet to hold open the door at her side of the car.

'It is my own private domain,' he continued, increasing her reluctance to alight, 'no one, not even Mistral, is allowed to visit me here without a personal invitation.'

Unnerved by his attitude of rising impatience, she obeyed his command and stepped out of the car into the dim, chilly atmosphere of a cavern gouged out of rock and connected to the apartment block by a swiftly ascending elevator.

'Why have you brought me here?' Her voice sounded thin and nervously quavering within the narrow confines of the elevator. 'You said you were taking me to your home!'

'This apartment is my home—or rather one of them,' he responded, then broke off when the lift glided to a halt on the topmost floor and the doors yawned wide, disgorging them into a corridor with cool, cream walls sweeping uninterrupted towards a solitary woodgrained door.

Her first impression of the interior of the apartment was one of spacious simplicity engendered by all-white walls, terracotta-tiled floors, a minimal amount of bric-à-brac, and just a couple of carefully placed watercolours.

But when Lucien drew back the shutters, flooding the apartment with sunshine reflecting from an expanse of sparkling blue sea, she saw that his preference for luxurious surroundings was stamped upon thickly upholstered chairs and couches, costly rugs, futuristic lamps, and every possible aid to labour-free living that could be accommodated within a compact, tastefully appointed kitchen.

'Let's go down to the beach for a swim,' he urged, loosening the knot of his tie before slipping off his jacket and tossing it on to a nearby chair.

Cherry turned aside, made to feel shy by the small act of intimacy, and in case he should suspect and find amusement in her embarrassment, hastened to point out:

'I've packed all my swimsuits and my luggage is still in the car.'

'You'll find a selection of new costumes in the bedroom through there . . .'

Her startled eyes swivelled in his direction, then quickly away from the sight of a shirt being whipped from his teak-brown, sweat-glistening torso.

Too shocked to argue, she flew towards the door he had indicated, banged it shut behind her, then leant against its panels, using her body as a trembling, panic-stricken buttress.

What a fool she had been to rely upon the comforting presence of Mistral and a houseful of servants! What on earth had possessed her to place her trust in a man who seemed proud of his playboy reputation!

'Hurry, *chérie*, I can't wait to get into the water!'

His rapped command, the suspicion that he would not hesitate to barge his way inside the bedroom to rout her out, sent her darting across the room towards a chest of drawers that seemed the likeliest-looking place in which to store swimsuits. She pulled a drawer right off its runners in her haste, then stared aghast at the pile of swimsuits, still wrapped in their original plastic bags, that had spilled on to the floor around her feet.

Grabbing the first plastic bag her fingers touched, she ran into an adjoining bathroom, stripped off her clothes, and in a matter of seconds was stepping inside a one-piece swimsuit which she sensed instinctively would be fashioned to fit a young, slim, curvaceous body.

Without stopping to replace the abandoned drawer she ran out of the bedroom, and came face to face with Lucien, whose outstretched hand seemed to supply proof that he had just been about to invade her privacy.

'At last!' he exploded wrathfully. 'A man could expire with frustration during the length of time it takes a woman to take off a few clothes!'

Cherry blushed, feeling completely eclipsed by wide shoulders and muscular chest tapering down to a lean, flat midriff and narrow hips encased in belted briefs stretching across his limbs like a supple black skin.

'Well, well!' His appraising look made her regret not sparing the time to search for a robe to cover up nakedness left by a leaf green swimsuit with daring cut-out panels that revealed a greater amount of cleavage than any skimpy bikini bra. 'I would never complain again about a woman's tardiness if I could count upon being rewarded with the breathtaking sight of pale rounded magnolia buds straining to burst from their leaf green prison. You have a beautiful body, Charity Sweet.' She felt as if his eyes were stripping the sparse leaf-green covering from her breasts. 'Full, rounded curves and supple limbs are said to be an accurate indication of maternal fruitfulness.'

Striving hard to suppress the scorching blush that not even an experienced actress could have produced at will, Cherry escaped his smouldering presence by responding to the call of a beckoning breeze that led her outside on to an arched patio that had a stairway curving towards a footpath inclining down the cliff face to the silver-sanded beach of a secluded cove. The patio, shut in on three sides by the curved walls of the building, contained a gridiron for cooking alfresco meals, a circular table complete with squat, rustic chairs, and a rattan beach chair, large enough for two, with a high arching back to act as protection from any freshening winds.

She headed towards it, intending to curl up among its cushions like a sun-worshipping kitten while Lucien had his swim, but she regretted her decision when, immediately she sat down, Lucien appeared strolling across to join her. She had to tuck in her feet to give him room to sit next to her, and hid clenched fists in a cushion as she pretended to ignore bold eyes continuing their assessment of the child-bearing potential of her half naked body.

Seated directly in the path of a heat-tempering breeze reaching from the sea to tease his black hair into ruffled tendrils, he seemed lazily disinclined to swim.

'Are you fond of children, *ma chérie*?'

Cherry sighed, sensing that, in the manner of a dog with a bone, he would refuse to let go until he had stripped the subject clean.

She chose her words carefully. 'As far back as I can remember our home seemed to be in a perpetual state of readiness for the arrival of a new baby. One of the things I missed most when I left was the ever-present smell of talcum powder, milk-stained bibs, rose hip syrup and gripe water.' She even managed a chuckle when dreamily basking in the sun with her eyes half closed, she indulged in the rare luxury of allowing her thoughts to drift homeward, to the sisters whose confidences she had shared and the mother who, in spite of her fear of her husband's displeasure, had tried in every way she could to persuade her firstborn child that she was loved.

'Even changing nappies can be made tolerable by the pleasant aftermath of holding a contentedly cooing, sweet-smelling baby in one's arms,' she confided, then lapsed into silence, browsing through treasured memories that excluded even Lucien's dominating presence from her mind.

But the sound of his forceful voice startled her heavy eyelids open, so that drowsy blue eyes were darkened by the shadow cast by his lowering head.

'I'd say that you are more in love with the vision of motherhood that you could ever be with a husband. In fact, I suspect, sweet Charity, that in spite of having been part of a large family, you have somehow missed out,' he frowned, 'have been denied your fair share of close human relationships. Even more than most females, you appear to *need* a child! Is that because you covet the absolute adoration that a mother inspires within a child who senses that she is completely vital to its survival? And how do you feel about the physical effects of bearing a child? In common with most men, I desire a woman to be beautiful and desirable—I could not bear to see someone I love transformed from a slim, sexy, girl into a bulging, easily nauseated monstrosity. Actresses should possess at least three essential qualities—a beautiful face, a shapely figure, and talent. Talent is a gift that can be safely depended upon to outlast one or even several broken marriages, but what about the more perishable qualities? Are you prepared to risk what could quite possibly turn out to be a brilliant career for the sake of ugly, restrictive pregnancy?'

When she had recovered wits that had been

scattered by his verbal onslaught, Cherry responded with an indignant denial.

'Pregnancy is not ugly!' She shot upright, prepared to defend this slight upon women who, with very rare exceptions, acquired a bloom that was unique to motherhood. 'I agree that in the context of ambition it could be restrictive, but of what value is spurious applause and the fleeting approval of critics compared with the worship of a child who gives its love freely, whether or not it is deserved!'

As suddenly as it had flared her fire of indignation died down, doused by a look of surprise that caused her to regret her foolish deviation from the lines of her original script, playing out a role completely different from the one she had so carefully rehearsed. Making an effort to avert questions she sensed were springing to Lucien's lips, she jerked her legs from under her and had actually gained her feet when his hand shot out to clamp a delaying band around her wrist.

'Sit down, *petite*,' he commanded smoothly. 'You cannot open a secret window and then bang it shut without giving me time for a further peep! What puzzles me is this. You must be a dedicated actress in search of work, otherwise you would not have chosen to visit Cannes during Film Festival week. Yet the remarks you have just made indicate a willingness to give up your career in favour of motherhood. Why? Have you become despondent about the success of your career? Is it because the parts you feel best qualified to play are not readily available?'

For a second she felt cornered. Then, playing

for time, she prised her wrist out of his grasp and
moved over towards a cane-roofed terrace to stand
poking a finger inside wooden louvres that pivoted
at a touch to deflect strong sunlight from
flowering pot plants. Now was the time to tell him
the truth! To admit that she could not act if her
life depended upon it, to tell him that she had been
forced into deceiving him by the weight of
gratitude she owed Diana; because the money he
had offered had been her salvation, and because of
the deep rapport she felt with Mistral, the
misguided, rejected adolescent who thought a
heart full of love was sufficient to ensure that she
was loved in return.

But the scars inflicted by Ryan's caustic tongue
were still too sensitive; the thought of enduring yet
again the lash of masculine contempt reduced her
to an artful coward.

'Working hard at makebelieve gives one less
opportunity to dwell upon what might have been,'
she told him calmly, hoping she had injected just
the right amount of nonchalance into her shrug.

'You mean constantly playing a studied part is a
barrier behind which you can hide the humiliation
inflicted by the man who let you down?'

She swung in his direction, wondering why every
oblique reference to Ryan should incur his deep
displeasure.

'Isn't every civilised person forced to act a part?'
she defended, tilting her head as he towered
towards her. 'Haven't *you*, *monsieur*, already
written a script, charted the plot of a play in which
you intend enacting the role of devoted lover with
sufficient conviction to dupe some unwary girl into
believing that you want her as a wife when all you

really require is a human machine that can be kept carefully maintained and regularly serviced in order to ensure the manufacture of a calculated number of perfect reproductions?'

Her intention had been to shame him, but his shrug of indifference confirmed that she had not succeeded.

'We French take a far more realistic view of marriage than the incautious English and consequently run far less risk of a *mésalliance*. The course of history has proved that the custom of arranging a marriage as one would negotiate a business merger cannot be improved upon—an undertaking for which keen judgment and an ability to drive a hard bargain are essential. French peasants, especially, cling tenaciously to the rule that every would-be bride must be supplied with a dowry. Not only must she be well provided with clothes and linen, she must offer in addition a substantial sum of money, scaled in accordance with the position held in society by her prospective bridegroom. The tyranny of the *dot* is absolute. Marriage is rarely a matter of mutual affection; it is still not uncommon—in rural districts, at least, where tradition is carefully nurtured—for a girl to meet her fiancé for the very first time on the day of their betrothal.'

His coldblooded, matter-of-fact attitude towards marriage had already been demonstrated, nevertheless Cherry found his remarks infuriating.

'Any girl willing to enter into marriage under such conditions deserves neither sympathy nor respect,' she snapped, 'merely contempt for her eagerness to be treated as a chattel, to offer years of loyalty, devotion, and compulsory childbearing in exchange for the indifference of a husband who has been conditioned, again by custom, to assume that infidelity is acceptable to his wife and *expected* of him by a male-orientated society that insists that a women must be kept tied while men are left to roam free! You French are a hypocritical race,' she condemned hotly, 'who condone unfaithfulness in men yet employ the excuse of religious taboo to deny women the right of divorce.'

'Such a code of conduct applies only to the middle and lower classes of our society,' Lucien corrected lazily, paying disconcerting attention to the agitated rise and fall of breasts threatening to overflow scanty leaf-green cups. 'Divorce is common among socialites. Indeed, its members are apt to marry, divorce and remarry with such confusing rapidity that one is forced to rely upon gossip columnists in order to keep track of who is married to whom. In retrospect, I think my previous condemnation of employees of the gutter press was perhaps a little harsh, for at least their scurrilous scribblings do help to prevent social gaffes being committed by absentee or ill-informed acquaintances. Even within my own very exclusive social circle there are suspected informers,' he amazed her by adding, 'members who are well placed, yet impoverished enough to accept payment from columnists in exchange for snippets of information confided by friends. There are spies everywhere, an underground network of informers with fingers so close to the pulse of social activity that it has been known for hints about a king's imminent abdication to be read with astonishment by diplomats in his own embassy. In fact,' his broad grin struck her as being ominously self-satisfied, 'I'm quite certain that seeds of speculation sown in the local branch of an international jewellers this very morning are already sprouting shoots and that by tomorrow morning, Mistral—who has a touching faith in the integrity of newspaper editors—will be convinced that my commitment to you is genuine. The report about our visit to that establishment is bound to include an estimated cost of the goods purchased as well as a description that will be correct down to the exact number of sapphire butterflies!'

Hastily Cherry turned aside to hide from his mocking eyes the spasm of inexplicable pain that had deepened her blue eyes to purple and made a trembling wreck of her mobile, easily-hurt mouth. She had known, of course, that there had to be some selfish motive behind every one of Lucien's actions, yet somewhere within the deep, secret recesses of her mind a spark of pleasure had been kindled by the gift whose perfection had appealed far more than its value. Just minutes earlier, undercover informers had been made the subject of his contempt—yet her quivering emotions could not differentiate between one who is prepared to accept payment in exchange for information, and one who used his wealth to achieve the maximum amount of personal publicity.

'Why aren't you wearing your delightful straw boater?'

She jerked with surprise when his hand slid beneath her chin to tilt her wilting head upright. 'It is not wise to linger bareheaded in the worst heat of the sun. And besides that,' he added with teasing charm, 'the hat is so very becoming.

Watching you wear it reminds me of days long past when the closest a boy was allowed to flirtatious involvement was to pull a girl's pigtails or to carry her books after school.'

Vaguely, Cherry swept a hand over a crown of hair turned molten by blazing sunshine, struggling to equate shy adolescence with an image of rampant male virility.

'I seem to have mislaid it,' she mumbled, then blushed when she was caught in the quizzical sight of eyes that seemed capable of reading her mind. 'Perhaps I've left it indoors—I'll go and see.'

But this avenue of escape was blocked when Lucien swerved in front of her so that teak-tanned shoulders were blotting out the sun.

'Why not join me for a swim?' he urged in a low, coaxing voice that turned both her will and her knees to water.

'I can't swim,' she gasped, lifting her eyes no higher than the tangle of fine dark hairs spread across his chest. 'I don't know how . . .'

'Then I'll teach you, *ma chérie*.' Though his words were indulgent his tone held a ring of laughter. 'Conditions could not be more perfect—warm sea, warm sun, and an extremely warm instructor who can hardly wait to begin the first lesson which ought to begin with an elementary caution: Keep your feet on the ground, sweet Charity, and until you are sure of your ability to cope with a strange new element don't be tempted to stray out of your depth!'

The caution echoed in her ears as continuously as a buoy-bell warning sailors to steer clear of dangerous undercurrents. But once, with her hand tightly clasped in his, Lucien had managed to persuade her to venture out far enough to allow gentle waves to froth warm as cream over her shoulders, her timidity was swamped by the strange new bliss of feeling her limbs grow weightless as she bobbed freely as a cork above a depth of deliciously cool blue sea.

Lucien adapted to his role of tutor with surprising seriousness, instructing patiently, firmly, and displaying a dedication to his pupil's cause that kept her too occupied with the task of following his instructions to allow any intrusion of shyness.

'Now, *petite*!' He clasped a steadying hand around each of her wrists, deciding that enough time had been spent frolicking, allowing her body to become accustomed to the buoyant effect of deep water. 'On the count of three, together we will duck our heads completely under water. I'll be holding you, so don't be afraid, you'll find it isn't quite so bad as you expected. Are you ready? One. Two. *Three!*'

Cherry's first instinct, immediately her head plunged beneath the surface, was to attempt to twist her wrists out of his grasp in order to fight her way back towards life-giving air. But for interminable seconds he kept her shackled, then released her so that she shot upwards to emerge spluttering and gasping, her unpinned hair a mass of molten gold spread across a blue silken cloak of sea.

'You look like an outraged mermaid,' he grinned when his seal-sleek head erupted beside her, 'one of the dangerous, alluring sirens said to have enticed seamen by the sweetness of their song to such a degree that the listeners forgot

everything and died of hunger! Before I succumb
to a similar fate, *ma chérie*,' when his grin widened
she blinked, dazzled by the whiteness of teeth
against his deep tan, 'will you trust me to tow you
safely across to the raft where I'll leave you to
float beneath the sun while I increase my appetite
with a final swim?'

Her eyes swivelled in the direction he had
indicated, to where a raft, anchored to the sea bed,
was rocking on a gentle swell. Nervously she eyed
the stretch of dividing water then, enticed by the
prospect of being left to luxuriate in sunbathed
solitude, she gulped, then placed her safety in his
hands with the willingness of a trustful child.

'Very well,' she nodded, 'what do I have to do?'

'Just remain completely relaxed.' Glinting admiration of her courage, he slid an arm across her
chest to grip her securely, then, keeping his body
turned sideways, he kicked out strongly, launching
them both into motion across the deep blue swell
of sea.

After the first few seconds of heart-beating
panic, calmness engendered by his cradling arm
and by the power behind the side stroke cleaving
them effortlessly through the water took over so
completely that she was able to earn his further
approval by leaning well back, allowing her legs to
float near the surface of the water.

It seemed to her that only a few minutes had
passed before she was called upon to follow his
crisp instruction:

'Get ready to grab hold of the handrail attached
to steps jutting beneath the water level.' She
twisted her head sideways and saw the raft
looming in front of her. Immediately her hand

closed around the rail Lucien switched his grip to her waist and held her steady while she groped for a foothold upon the first submerged rung before heaving herself up on to the second, third, then finally on to the swaying, rope-woven surface of the raft.

Ignoring the steps, Lucien placed the palms of his hands flat on the floor of the raft and with one easy movement heaved out of the water to stretch his dripping, muscular frame alongside her.

'It puzzles me why men, who are reluctant even to witness the trauma of childbirth, should be surprised by the discovery that courage forms part of the female composition, yet invariably we are,' he confessed with a look of approval that caused Cherry's toes to curl.

With a sigh of contentment he rolled over to allow fingers of sunshine to massage the planes and hollows formed by back muscles flexing sinuously as a cat's beneath a soaking pelt, inching closer and closer until she could feel the cool hard length of his body pressing limb to limb, pore to pore, flesh to alert, vitally aroused flesh . . .

She remained still as a mouse, listening to his low, even breathing roaring deafeningly in her ears; feeling nerve-ends rearing out towards him, rendered completely disorientated by unfamiliar sensations coursing through her body, an inexplicable soaring, peaking, then plunging into troughs that could have no possible connection with the gently undulations of the almost motionless raft.

When his fingers began tracing a line of fire across her damp shoulder she surrendered with a sigh to the inevitable, and made no effort to resist even when he rolled her over on her back and slid one leaf-green strap off her shoulder. Weakness shot through her body at the sight of his tense, hungry expression and a mouth hovering with momentary anticipation. Then her lashes swept down to hide unbearable shyness just as his lips descended, light as a butterfly's kiss upon newly unfurled petals . . .

It took time for her to acknowledge the humiliating fact that her craving for more was not to be appeased. For an eternity of minutes she lay waiting with her eyes still closed, urging his vibrant body nearer, longing for her raging thirst to be quenched with bitter-sweet kisses. Then slowly her lashes lifted so that puzzled, pleading eyes could question the abrupt dousing of his devouring fire.

His profile was etched against the skyline, his head half turned, peering out to sea as if anxious to identify the occupants of a boat bobbing a few hundred yards' distance from the raft. Even before he spoke, the sight of his grimly satisfied smile caused her hot, racing blood to run cold.

'I hope the camera being used by the *paparazzi* is equipped with a telescopic lens,' he laughed scornfully. 'The fools are probably congratulating themselves on a clever bit of sleuthing, unaware that all day long they have been following clues dropped conspicuously as a paper trail around every prestigious store in Cannes.'

Cherry winced, pained by the reminder of a flashbulb exploding in her face as she had paraded in a fur chosen deliberately to excite speculation.

'Tomorrow, all the gossip column devotees will be discussing at length the Duc de Marchiel's mysterious fiancée! Now is the time for us to go to ground,' he decided thoughtfully. 'Paris should provide an ideal hideout. When we return from our illicit weekend no one, not even Mistral, will dare to cast doubts upon the authenticity of our unheralded betrothal!'

CHAPTER EIGHT

THEY travelled to Paris in an executive jet which Lucien—who Cherry would have been willing to wager had never spent so much as an hour straphanging during a rush hour—averred was a necessity rather than a luxury in an era when half the world's population appeared to be constantly on the move.

On their way to the airport he had stopped to buy newspapers, and after ensuring that she was safely strapped into a seat inside a cabin fitted out to resemble rather a luxuriously appointed salon than the interior of an aircraft, he had tossed them into her lap before entering the cockpit to prepare for take-off.

'The journey will not take long,' his sharp eyes had quizzed her expressionless features. 'I know your French is not good, nevertheless, by the time we reach Paris I'm sure you will have managed to decipher enough of the gossip column text to agree that my plan is working out well.'

But the plane had been airborne for less than ten minutes when Cherry found it necessary to unbuckle her seat-belt and stagger across to a cabinet in search of a stiff, restorative drink. Her ability to speak his language was limited and her understanding of the written word even more so, but no expertise had been needed to interpret the blown-up, nakedly explicit message transmitted by a photograph emblazoned across an inner page of the first newspaper she had opened.

With shaking fingers she poured a measure of brandy from a crystal decanter, then gulped down the drink until her glass was empty. The bite of raw spirit upon her unseasoned tongue took her breath away, but shock still remained, the shock of seeing herself posed in a scene of apparent debauchery, a waist-length shot of two naked figures entwined in a torrid embrace, with Lucien's unmistakable profile frozen in swooping descent upon her upturned, blatantly inviting mouth ...

She trembled back into her seat and with a shudder of repugnance returned to the newspaper to begin painfully translating its scurrilous text.

Jet-setting socialite Lucien Tarascon, Duc de Marchiel, has a mysterious young beauty installed in his love-nest—the notorious eyrie spread out across the entire top floor of an exclusive block of flats built for celebrities along a stretch of coast near Antibes known as Millionaires' Row! Monsieur le Duc is reported to have been seen seducing his new companion with gifts of expensive clothes, shoes, and fabulous furs, as well as a suite of sapphire jewellery which, it was hinted, has been purchased to mark their engagement. Despite the handsome playboy's aversion to publicity, rumours about his new love are following strongly in his wake. Some say that the Duc's companion is a German princess, but Riviera socialites insist that she is a blue-blooded member of the English aristo-

*cracy and that their romantic idyll in Antibes is
quite likely an advance honeymoon. The Duc's
ward, Mistral Peissel, who up until the arrival
of the mysterious newcomer had been his
constant companion, was asked her opinion of
the liaison, but declined to comment. It would
appear, however, that the above picture, taken
yesterday, renders speculation superfluous!
Watch this space for further advance information
about the intriguing alliance that has set Riviera
society rocking on its heels!*

Half an hour later Cherry tossed the papers
aside, sickened by constant references to Lucien's
reputation as a womaniser; his playboy image, his
confirmed bachelor status, and most of all, by the
hints and innuendoes directed towards herself; the
question marks drawn invisibly behind each
reference to her conduct, and the accompanying
photograph that appeared to supply only incriminating answers.

She slumped back in her seat and closed her
eyes, struggling to come to terms with the fact that
she had been tricked into notoriety by a man
without scruples, one who had gained her trust by
displaying a chivalrous determination to protect
his ward's reputation, then had proceeded with
calculated cunning to destroy her own good name.

By the time she felt the plane dipping and then
losing height as if preparing to land, her
conscience had forced her to conclude that she had
no option but to carry out to its conclusion the job
for which she had already been paid. Her mind felt
numbed, she felt physically scarred for life, her
body robbed of something rare and precious—and

yet conversely enriched by an experience that had jolted her alive, leaving her emotions humming and vibrating with the continuity of a newly switched-on dynamo.

A hired Lamborghini was waiting for them at the airport. When Lucien helped her into the passenger seat before sliding behind the wheel to direct the nose of the limousine in the direction of Paris, Cherry braced mentally for an inquisition, having already decided that it was imperative that he should never be allowed to guess how distressed she had been made to feel, how cheapened, how used, how lacking in both morals and discretion.

'Well, *ma chérie*, did you find the reports in the newspapers entertaining?' Lightly he tossed the question her way, giving most of his attention to negotiating a roundabout before cruising slowly along a slip road, waiting for a gap to appear in the motorway traffic.

Taking advantage of the fact that his concentration was fully occupied, Cherry took time to compose her thoughts so that she might successfully emulate the example of Diana, who crept inside the skin of each role she was given and allowed her characters' thoughts, words and actions to dominate her entire existence until the final curtain had been lowered.

'The headlines were certainly eye-catching,' she agreed, 'and the picture even more so.' She relaxed against the sumptuous upholstery, striving to project the air of a languid Camille. 'An experienced publicity manager couldn't have managed better to turn a unknown starlet into an overnight celebrity. I feel I've become one of the small international elite of girls whose close associations with the wealthy and famous are closely reported in the society columns.'

High-class madames, she could have added, *dedicated to the quest after men willing to drip-feed their egos with ermine and pearls!*

The fast speeding car swerved fractionally when Lucien took his eyes off the road just long enough to cast her a quick, searching glance.

'So you have no objection to baring your breasts in public providing the exercise results in financial benefits,' he growled, then uttered a short laugh of disbelief. 'You are an even better actress than I had imagined, *ma petite*. Last night in my flat, when you locked yourself inside a bedroom and refused to come out even for a bite of supper, I was misguided enough to imagine that the incident with the *paparazzi* had caused you much distress, that your sensitive feelings had been outraged. *Merci, mademoiselle*,' he mocked savagely, 'for relieving my mind of groundless worry. I shall remember in future that, in common with the rest of the attractive, unattached girls who are always to be found in the world's most luxurious playgrounds, you regard scruples as mere constrictions, to be discarded with the same lack of resistance you show to abandoning the upper half of a swimsuit!'

It was just as well that he appeared neither to expect nor to require any response that would have had to have been forced through a throat so tightly blocked she found difficulty in swallowing. So she remained silent, cloaking her misery in dignified aloofness, wondering why his profile should have adopted a mask of iron, why hands steering the car competently through a mad rush

of cars that appeared to be driven by suicidal
maniacs should be showing a white-knuckled grip
on the steering wheel.

She shivered, caught in the blast of super-
efficient air-conditioning that made driving such a
pleasure in the south but which had been rendered
superfluous by a cooler northern temperature.
Then as they drove through the outskirts of Paris
it began raining, a steady grey drizzle that caused
her vision to be interrupted by constantly arcing
windscreen wipers, rendering what little she could
see of the world's most colourful and lively capital
dank and depressing.

Not even the deferential welcome accorded to
them upon their arrival at a grand hotel with
reception rooms panelled in wall-to-wall gilt
mirroring lending an illusion of acres of space
crammed with sofas and tables being navigated by
an army of soft-footed waiters, was successful in
raising her drooping spirits.

Patiently, she stood aside while Lucien checked
in at the reception desk, too unfamiliar with the
procedure to question the correctness of his
signing the register on her behalf, and giving no
thought at all to their accommodation arrangements until, after they had been swept aloft in a
noiseless lift, they were ushered inside what was
obviously a penthouse suite. Immediately she
rounded to voice a protest, only to be silenced by
Lucien's warning frown. But the moment the door
closed behind a well-tipped porter, she trained on
him blue eyes flashing brilliant with indignation.

'Because it has always been my policy to make
the best of what can't be altered, I made no
objection to being forced to spend last night alone

with you in your flat. Nevertheless, it was never my intention to allow such an arrangement to become permanent. Please,' she drew herself tall, 'oblige me by removing yourself and your luggage out of my room, *monsieur*—or alternatively,' she cast a nervous glance around the magnificent sitting-room, 'instruct the management that I'm to be provided with a separate room.'

'*Ciel*! Pious Charity! If I did not know you better I would say that you were aptly named!'

She faltered into retreat when he began a swift approach, but was trapped at the rear when her shoulders made contact with solid wooden panels. Quickly, he pounced, pinning her like a fluttering butterfly against the unyielding door.

'You are bound by an unwritten agreement to carry out whatever duties are demanded of you by your employer,' he reminded her curtly. 'The moment you accepted payment for such duties our contract became valid. However, as your working conditions are slightly unusual, I am prepared to add sugar to the pill so that you will find my constant presence less indigestable.'

Cherry stared blankly, unwilling to struggle in case he should decide to subdue her resistance by increasing his tormenting hold upon a body that was reacting like that of a fallen angel to the touch of Alichino, the devil of allurement.

'What do you mean?' she gasped, her lips drained bloodless by a reminder of a cynical mouth that had crushed through a barrier of shyness to scorch her dry of innocence.

'I mean, Charity Sweet, that for an actress you possess a shockingly ill-equipped wardrobe and an equally conspicuous lack of grooming—omissions which, if society is to believe what we wish it to believe, must be rectified immediately. Don't bother to unpack the carousel of separates whose diverse appearances have left me dizzy. I have a friend, Cécile, a high priestess of haute couture, who can supply you with outfits, shoes, lingerie, in fact everything an aristocratic impostor is likely to need.'

'As no doubt she has proved when called upon to equip previous members of your harem!' The caustic remark flew from her lips before she had time to consider the consequence.

'Is that how you see yourself?' His darkly scored eyebrows soared, then drew together in a scowl. 'If slaves are supposed to pleasure their masters,' he threatened grimly, drawing her slowly towards him, 'then once again I must admit to being less than satisfied with the manner in which you carry out your duties. I think perhaps it might be wise,' he murmured against the pale cool curve of her cheek, 'if I were to dispose of all danger of future conflict by demonstrating the method I favour for curbing rebellion.'

'Don't . . .!'

Cherry pleaded to be spared the punishment spelled out in flame against the depths of eyes that looked ready to devour.

But without a sign of compassion Lucien captured her parted lips beneath his own, pulling her closer until her head was bent back over his arm while sensuously he ran light, stroking fingers over straining breasts, then slowly down to her thighs. Dormant nerves leapt into life wherever he touched, so that when his leisurely chastisement had been concluded she felt that

every chaste secret part of her had been baptised
by fire.

'Regard that as a lesson against the blight of
rancour!'

Roughly her tutor set her aside, looking almost
as shaken as his distraught pupil. 'If ever again
you should feel tempted to adopt the attitude of a
shrew, think about the orange trees lining the
Riviera verges, heavy with fruit that looks ripe
with promise, yet shunned, left to rot ever since
thieves discovered that flesh that appears inviting
can often taste bitter!'

As he escorted her out of the hotel into the grey
damp streets of Paris, Cherry felt as drained as
Diana had often appeared after being put through
her emotional paces at drama school, called upon
to portray ecstasy and pain, to switch from
weeping to laughter, from loving to suffering,
barely given time to draw breath between the
cessation of one emotion and the commencement
of the next.

Landmarks made familiar by picture postcards
leapt into reality as Lucien drove through streets
milling with tourists climbing steps leading up to a
white church he said was the Sacré Coeur;
pointing a mass of cameras towards the Eiffel
Tower and the Arc de Triomphe; looking shocked,
furtive, daring and openly amused by explicitly
immoral invitations being issued around the
sleazier parts of Montmartre, then suitably pious
as they pored over tourist maps and itineraries
demanding a visit to the imposing Notre Dame.

Cherry felt great relief when he steered the car
away from the race-track ambience of the
Champs-Elysées and into a quiet little thoroughfare

that had been turned into a community of discreet fashion houses and expensive-looking boutiques.

'A word of caution.' He broke her absorption as he drew the car to a standstill adjacent to steps leading upwards to an imposing door. 'Do not expect to be consulted about your choice of outfits. Cécile's eye for colour and design is infallible, she is an artist who approaches each new client as a blank . canvas—first sketching an outline, then deciding upon the shades and textures she will choose to produce an eventual masterpiece. Each creation is given an appropriate title. Many of her clients are unknown to her by name,' he mused, guiding her reluctant feet up the flight of stone steps until he was within reach of a hand moulded from iron, its knuckles clenched in readiness to rap a demand for entry against wooden door panels, 'princesses and artistes alike respond with alacrity when christened with names such as L'Allumeuse; La Belle Chanteuse, or La Jeune Tigresse.'

Though Cherry was in no doubt about Lucien's social worth, his status was amply confirmed by the almost slavish obsequiousness that greeted his appearance once they had been bowed across the threshold by a liveried doorman.

'Oh, Monsieur le Duc! How nice to see you again!' An extremely soignée assistant of indeterminate age cast a covert glance at Cherry while advancing to concentrate fullsome attention upon Lucien. 'Madame Cécile will be delighted to learn of your arrival. Allow me to lead the way to her salon, *monsieur—mademoiselle*. We have been instructed never to leave Monsieur le Duc de Marchiel waiting!'

Cherry's preoccupation with the task of deciding whether Lucien's familiarity with such names as the Firebrand, the Beautiful Songstress and the Young Tigress had come about because of close association with their owners was superseded by awe when they were shown into a salon furnished with exquisite taste and priceless objets d'art that formed a perfect background for the dainty old lady wearing a satin dress exactly the colour and sheen of her silver hair. Cherry had no doubt whatsoever that the personage enthroned with queenlike dignity upon a high-backed chair padded and covered in pastel-shaded tapestry was Cécile.

'Lucien, *mon bon ami*!' She raised a cheek to meet his kiss of greeting. 'Take pity upon an old lady's loneliness by promising to have lunch with me? And your young friend, of course . . .'

She turned diamond-bright eyes upon Cherry, who shrank momentarily, then relaxed, warming to the twinkle of genuine goodwill outshining a hint of Gallic severity.

'We would be delighted.' Without prior consultation, he accepted on Cherry's behalf. 'Because of your well known predilection for becoming acquainted with prospective patrons before agreeing to include them in your exclusive clientele, I have made no plans for lunching elsewhere.'

'You make me sound like a witch who is liable to employ real live models as targets for her pins of disapproval,' Cécile scolded with asperity. 'First of all, introduce me to your young friend, then sit down and allow me to enjoy without interruption the sight of a blush which, having survived the turbulence of adolescence, is almost certain to attain sweet maturity.'

Surprisingly, Lucien accepted the rebuke with a smile that held no trace of resentment, then displayed implicit trust in Cécile's discretion by introducing candidly.

'Cécile, *mon amie*, I would like to present Miss Charity Sweet, an English actress who has kindly agreed to help me out of an embarrassing situation by posing for a while as my fiancée. The scene of deception has been set, the dialogue rehearsed until the leading lady is word-perfect—all she lacks is a wardrobe of clothes designed to add a final flair to her undeniable talent.'

'Talent? Talent for what . . .?'

Cherry's blush leapt to the prodding of old eyes too wise to be deceived.

'For impersonation—what else?' Lucien's raised eyebrows seemed to indicate that he was finding Cécile unusually obtuse. Predictably, the spirited old madame bridled.

'My creations are designed to be worn by people, not by puppets!' she snapped. 'If costumes are what you require, then I suggest you approach a theatrical outfitter whose skill lies in an ability to conceal from an audience the sincerity that my garments are exclusively designed to reveal!'

Evidence of the strength of affection they shared was made plain by the docility with which Lucien accepted Cécile's rebuke and by the effort she put into re-establishing good relations while they shared what she termed a light snack of quail, lobster, wild strawberries and champagne.

Cherry played a little part in the conversation, but was content merely to sit back and be entertained by the conversational ball being tossed lightly to and fro between the pair who, in spite of the discrepancy in their ages, seemed inextricably bound by ties of deep and abiding friendship. However, the blush that had never quite faded from her cheeks since her shocked encounter with the incriminating photograph returned in full force when Cécile observed a trifle dryly:

'According to this morning's newspapers, *mon cher*, you are continuing to supply most of the fodder needed to feed the insatiable appetite of the *paparazzi*.'

Cecile had not so much as glanced her way, yet Cherry felt certain that she was aware of the shiver that had taken her relaxed body unawares.

'Unfortunately, yes,' Lucien nodded briefly. 'Sensational publicity is one of the penalties of being regarded by columnists as a "big name". But I hope,' he reminded her lightly, 'true friends will refuse to believe me capable of behaving as badly as the headlines suggest. I make no effort to hide the fact that I like to have fun, that I am happy to be alive, but the playboy label that I appear to be stuck with is a piece of highly exaggerated fiction. Indeed, until very recently I had virtually given up late nights and night clubs and had practically become a stranger to café society.'

'*Pauvre petit!*' Though Cecile's smile was sympathetic the look she sparkled across the table was slightly teasing. 'I know how you must resent unwarranted intrusion into your affairs, how lack of privacy makes you angry and frustrated—nevertheless, I find it impossible to picture you living the life of a hermit, shunning friends completely. In fact, did you not imply only moments ago that your young companion,' she smiled at Cherry, 'is being used as a barrier to protect you from the attentions of some over-zealous female? *Non, non, mon cher*, you must try not to mind if people stop and stare. Your exotic Riviera tan and handsome features are very easy on the eye—as I'm certain Mademoiselle Cherry will agree?'

Without prior warning Cherry became conscious of two pairs of eyes swivelling in her direction as a keenly interested old lady and a derisively smiling man waited for her response to the embarrassing question.

'Oh ... er ... yes, I'm certain you are right, *madame*,' she stammered truthfully, then concluded in a breathless rush, 'It can be no great hardship to a man to be considered one of the world's greatest lovers.'

Immediately Cecile laughed aloud and an angry tide of colour swept beneath Lucien's tan she realised that quite unintentionally her remark had projected a note of censure. This suspicion was confirmed when Cécile gleefully seized the instrument so unwittingly forged to use it as a weapon of teasing malice.

'A back-handed compliment indeed!' she chuckled, obviously enjoying the rare experience of seeing Lucien's ego deflated. 'I think I agree with *la jeune demoiselle*'s discreet implication that any man who wishes to avoid becoming the subject of sensational headlines must maintain a steady relationship with one woman, preferably a wife. Marriage adds balance to a man's life. Just knowing that there is someone with whom he can spend a quiet evening at home, who will

understand his wish for an early night, who will
share his hopes, his fears and his ambitions, can
change the outlook of even the most dedicated
Casanova. *Oui, mon cher*, I definitely share
Cherry's view that marriage would be good for
you, and should you happen to fall in love with
your wife then so much the better! To love and be
loved is an experience even more fulfilling then a
creative career.' Her expression grew suddenly
pensive. 'A loving companion can turn the most
mundane occupation into a beautiful shared
experience.'

Cherry sensed Lucien's annoyance when he rose
to take his leave with the curt observation:

'A typically feminine solution to a bachelor's
problem! But fortunately I don't have time to get
lonely, and also, probably because I am hard to
please and easily annoyed by unpredictable female
behaviour, I decided long ago that the sort of
deep-lasting love wives expect of a husband is
mere fallacy—a stick used by woman to stir a
man's conscience!

'*Au revoir*, Cécile,' he stooped to place a
displeased kiss upon her cheek. 'Please don't
disturb yourself, we will see ourselves out.'

Hastening to respond to his beckoning wave,
Cherry rose to her feet, then hesitated, looking
from one to the other in utter bewilderment. Then
as if the perceptive old lady had read her mind she
consoled softly:

'How strange you must find the ways of the
abrupt and often arrogant Provençal, *ma petite*!
You come to a fashion house expecting no doubt
to be asked to choose from a selection of dresses,
then find yourself being asked to leave without

having seen so much as a bolt of silk or a sketched design. Would you believe that your measurements have been carefully noted?' She ran an experienced eye over Cherry's figure, then nodded as if satisfied with previous calculations. 'Hip measurements standard for one of average height,' she confirmed almost to herself, 'a waistline requiring tucks and full rounded breasts that will be displayed to perfection by a décolleté neckline. Leave the selection of outfits in my hands,' she urged. 'I promise, *ma belle ange*, that you will not be disappointed. During the next couple of weeks my staff will be expending all available time and energy upon meeting the bulk of your requirements, but meanwhile I have in stock a few suitable garments needing only minor alterations that will be delivered to your hotel before evening.

'*Au revoir, ma petite.*' Much to Cherry's surprise and pleasure Cécile proffered a cheek for a farewell kiss and when she stooped to oblige murmured low, so that Lucien could not overhear, 'Thank goodness we women are not bound to dress according to the company we keep, otherwise at this moment,' she cast a wicked look in the direction of Lucien's impatiently pacing presence, 'I should feel forced to supply you with a set of the slinky black leathers currently in vogue with followers of flint-eyed, rebellious hell's angels!'

CHAPTER NINE

ALLOWING Cherry no time to browse around the extensive ground-floor boutique, Lucien cut short her awed examination of a black lizard skin cabin trunk with matching luggage, a fascinating display of costume jewellery, and an eye-catching collection of shoes fashioned from supple leather—the cost of each pair, she estimated, equivalent to more than her monthly earnings—by marching her outside and retaining his grip upon her arm until they reached the car parked close to the pavement.

'I assume that while we are waiting for Cécile to wave a magic wand that will transform an actress into an embryo *duchesse*, you wish to go sightseeing?' he commented acidly, opening the car door and inviting her, with a wave of his hand, to be seated inside.

Wondering what she had said or done to provoke his attitude of savage displeasure, she stooped to obey, then hesitated with one foot hovering over the sill before withdrawing it back on to the pavement and slowly straightening.

'Naturally I'm eager to explore Paris,' she admitted, an impulsive flare of rebellion quelled by the imperious lift of demanding eyebrows. 'But must we travel by car? Couldn't we just . . . walk?' she faltered, her enthusiasm deflated by an incongruous mental image of an aristocratic socialite wandering like a rubbernecking tourist around the streets of Paris.

'*Walk?*' Lucien placed incredulous stress upon the word that fell as alien from his lips as some obscure foreign language. 'To tour Paris on foot could take days! Do you realise, I wonder, that if one were to spend only a couple of minutes in front of each exhibit it would take all of six weeks to get round the Louvre?'

Leaping to take advantage of a slight inflection in his voice that seemed to indicate that the world-weary Duc had become momentarily intrigued, Cherry assured him eagerly!

'I'd prefer not to follow the usual tourist trail. Places such as the Moulin Rouge, the Champs-Elysées, and the Place de la Concorde have been so extensively publicised that I feel I know them well enough already. What I'd really like to do is to explore behind the scenes, to become acquainted with the true people of Paris by travelling with them on the Métro, listening while they bargain in the market place, watch them eat, drink, and shop in their everyday, garlic-flavoured, wine-soaked, accordion-playing environment.'

'Are you quite certain that will be enough to satisfy your urge to return to basics? After all, we could be really off-beat by hiring a couple of bicycles.'

His dry rebuke brought a lump of disappointment to her throat. With head drooping and downcast lashes forming a silken gold barrier against a welling flood of regret, she managed to murmur an apology.

'I'm sorry, it was a stupid and highly

romanticised notion anyway. Let's forget it, shall we?'

Stooping to enter the car, she was pulled up short by the grip of his hand upon her elbow, and his sigh of resigned surrender.

'Very well, just this once I'll try to subdue my tendency to dominate, and allow you to do things your way. Come, let's look for the nearest Métro station!'

Five rushed, breathless, exciting minutes later she was skipping, with a hand clasped in his, down steps plunging deep into the bowels of the city, where fast, efficient trains were speeding through underground caverns splaying like the tentacles of an octopus towards the suburbs and beyond. In a daze of happy anticipation she waited while Lucien stood surrounded by a class of chattering schoolchildren, queueing for a *carnet* of tickets, then felt her heart had suddenly sprouted wings when, as he strode to join her, she saw that a broad grin of enjoyment had displaced the customary mask of boredom from his world-weary features.

She knew he was mocking her plebeian taste, yet felt not the slightest bit offended when, mocking the triumph of a shrewd French housewife, he waved two books of tickets under her nose.

'These entitle us to clock up *unlimited* mileage during the next four days! The whole of Paris is at your disposal, *ma chérie*, so choose a destination from the map of the Métro displayed on the wall behind you.'

She spun round to face a bewildering map of colourful lines connecting a multitude of stations with unfamiliar place names. She was just about ready to confess to confusion when she heard a query directed by the harassed-looking teacher in charge of the schoolchildren towards a passing official.

'*Quelle direction dois-je prendre pour le Bois de Boulogne?*'

Cherry spun on her heel, deciding on impulse: 'Let's follow the children!'

For a second Lucien looked taken aback, then, with a shrug that communicated an 'in for a penny in for a pound' resignation, he agreed with a conspicuous lack of enthusiasm:

'Very well, if it will please you, *ma chérie.*'

Pleasure was too lukewarm an emotion to describe the delightful experience of being crushed into seats within a compartment filled with laughing, boisterous yet fairly well behaved children whose enjoyment of the outing was so infectious that Cherry was able to relax completely, feeling as if she too had been freed for a while from the demands and restrictions imposed by a figure of authority.

She had to smile when, as the novelty of the journey waned, the children began foraging inside haversacks holding packed lunches—hunks of cheese, sticks of crusty bread, fruit and wide-necked thermos flasks containing favourite brands of liquid nourishment. A precocious young blonde girl whose admiring stare had been fixed upon Lucien since the moment of their departure began wrestling unsuccessfully with the screw-top cup of her flask, then fluttered a look of helpless appeal towards him.

'*Aidez-moi, s'il vous plaît, monsieur?*'

Cherry experienced a spasm of sympathy for the

child, who fell immediately under the spell of his charming smile.

'*Volontiers, mademoiselle.*' With a flick of his wrist he loosened the top, then inched slightly aside as he handed it over, obviously wary of liquid being slopped over his immaculate lightweight suit.

'Let me help!' In a bid to avert disaster Cherry took charge of the flask and began pouring hot liquid into the cup clasped between the schoolgirl's palms.

'Mm, it smells delicious!' she sniffed when a mouthwatering aroma drifted beneath her nostrils.

'Maman makes soup from just plain mashed carrots mixed with herbs and milk,' the child confided proudly. 'She can make one with onions too, and as a special treat I am sometimes allowed to have bread, toasted and sprinkled with grated cheese, floating on the top, just like Papa. Do you make soup for your children, *madame*?' Her eyes swivelled towards Lucien as she sipped daintily. 'And do you make *croutons* with grated cheese especially for Monsieur?'

The girl had said nothing to cause her embarrassment, yet when Cherry's eyes met Lucien's mocking glance she blushed, remembering the night of their dinner date when he had initiated her into the local custom and also into the strange new experience of feeling cossetted and expertly charmed. Luckily, their abrupt arrival at the station where they were due to alight caused an uproar amongst the children, and she was able to cover up her confusion by assisting the panicking girl to pour the remainder of her soup back into the thermos and replacing the lid securely before stuffing it into her haversack.

'*Merci, madame—monsieur,*' the child waved a wistful goodbye as she was being ushered on to the platform to become part of a crocodile.

'*Je vous en prie,*' Lucien responded with a courteous bow that caused the girl to preen with the pleasure of knowing herself envied by her fellow pupils. 'I hope you have a very pleasant day.'

'I've no doubt she will,' Cherry gurgled, waving until their starry-eyed young friend had been shepherded out of sight. 'Unlike men, females, whatever their age, treasure throughout their entire lifetime the memory of their first heady sip of infatuation.'

'You appear to be speaking from experience, *ma chérie.*' His drawl was lazy but his gaze intent. 'Tell me truthfully, can you really remember the very first time you fell in love?'

'Of course I can!' she burbled without thought, then gasped with shock, tricked by the pleasure of the moment into acknowledging a truth that previously had been kept submerged deep in her subconscious. Her agitation was so great, her mind so confused, she was barely conscious of his voice grating with renewed savagery.

'*Mon Dieu!* Up until this moment I had never really been able to believe that when a woman has no other burden she will take up a load of stones! What martyrs you all are!' Lucien jerked, his impatient eyes roving her pale, pinched face. 'You must learn to discard painful memories, reject all thoughts of the man who has hurt you so much that you flinch at the very mention of his name!'

Vaguely Cherry returned his angry stare with eyes completely devoid of sparkle—deep, blue, fathomless as the sea cradling the raft that had rocked her into a mood of rapture which her untutored emotions had failed to recognise as love . . .

Regretting the misunderstanding that had caused him to bracket unrequited love with the stepfather who had caused her so much unhappiness, yet unable to bear the idea of introducing Ryan's name into the conversation, Cherry made a determined effort to soothe Lucien's ruffled temper, and as gradually his stern mouth relaxed into a smile and he began responding less tersely to her forced chatter she was rewarded by the knowledge that she was succeeding.

They entered a huge park and began strolling along paths bordered with shrubs and trees, past boating lakes and restaurants and open-air cafés where accordionists were playing and couples dancing.

'The Bois, as it is known to locals, is the remainder of an old forest left to run wild until Louis Napoleon III turned its neglected solitude from a place favoured by duellists and people of dubious character into a place of relaxation and fun for the people of Paris. One of its main attractions, which we will visit later,' he promised with a smile, 'is the Parc de Bagatelle, a walled English garden made famous by its magnificent displays of flowers. But then again,' he teased down into eyes that had recaptured their glorious blue sparkle as they darted this way and that, approaching each change of scene with the anticipation of an eager child, 'perhaps the Jardin d'Acclimatation would be more to your liking—a garden of zoology,' he explained when she looked puzzled, 'you can just see the roof of the restaurant through those trees,' he pointed. 'Would you care for some refreshment?'

When she eagerly accepted he guided her in the direction of an attractive building with a low-slung thatched roof that lent it the appearance of an old farmhouse. As they walked into the surrounding compound ducks and chickens foraged for crumbs around their feet and amiable-looking goats and plump caged rabbits eyed them hopefully, made greedy by a surfeit of titbits.

Inside, the seating arrangements were made up of long wooden benches ranged the length of tables left uncluttered by tablecloths and other unnecessary refinements.

'What a lovely atmosphere!' Cherry beamed.

He smiled agreement and waited until they were settled into seats left vacant next to a voluble French family who were using laughter and amusing conversation as an aid to digestion, before handing her a menu.

'Just a coffee for me, thank you.' She waved it away. 'I don't want anything to spoil the memory of the luxurious lunch Cécile provided.'

'A very light lunch,' he reminded her, making her heart skip a beat by emulating the example of the rest of the men seated around the table by shrugging off his jacket, removing his tie, and loosening three top shirt buttons so that the collar fell away revealing a wide vee of tanned chest contrasting strongly as dark coffee against the cream silk folds of his shirt.

'The animals will be disappointed if you don't feed them,' he nodded towards an ancient goat and a very tame sheep meandering towards their table.

Cherry cast a glance over her shoulder, then, looking highly amused, decided with an engaging twinkle!

'Well, in that case I'd better have a cake with my coffee.'

'Come with me to the pâtisserie counter and choose your own.' Lucien rose to his feet, his expression looking sorely tried, yet laughing eyes assured her that he was only pretending.

Her mouth began watering as soon as she came within sniffing distance of a glass-covered counter that was a paradise of pastries—juicy tarts fresh from the oven; fragrant honey and nut slices; sweet, coloured frostings and soft cakes wallowing in rum-flavoured syrup. After much deliberation she chose a flaky cone with a custard filling for the sheep, a cream-filled sponge cake for the almost toothless goat, and—because she had recaptured once more the abandon of a schoolgirl rebel—a doughnut for herself to dunk in her coffee.

With the sheep and goat trailing in their wake, they returned to their table, then collapsed into helpless laughter at the sight of a cat and a dog waiting patiently, obviously having become expert at singling out customers likely to provide them with sustenance. The dog, especially, seemed to share Lucien's preference for chocolate biscuits, and showed his gratitude by flopping down at his feet to fasten huge adoring eyes upon his benefactor, remaining even when the last crumb had been devoured and the rest of his band had wandered away.

'You two look made for each other!' Cherry

teased, unaware of a faint trail of jam streaked across her chin. 'Are you fond of animals, Lucien?' she cocked her head enquiringly, wishing he could always wear the informal uniform of a cheerful peasant rather than the mantle of an aloof duke.

'Very,' he nodded, bending to stroke his hand over the mongrel's silken pelt. 'Little islands make small prisons; one cannot look at the sea without wishing for the wings of a swallow. Once, before I was old enough to be sent away to boarding school, my dog was my only companion. It created for me an atmosphere of *bonne entente*—living happily together—which I have never been fortunate enough to recapture.'

'Perhaps you should buy a puppy to replace the devoted companion you lost,' she suggested, sobered by an insight into a lonely, neglected childhood.

'Or perhaps, as you suggested to Cécile, a wife would be a more advantageous choice,' Lucien charged, reverting suddenly to a light note of mockery tempered with steel. 'As you were the one who broached the idea that has since been teasing my mind, I consider I am entitled to demand your further assistance. I bought myself a fiáncée, *ma chérie*—now tell me where I am likely to find an equally obliging wife for sale?'

The dimple that had danced at the corner of Cherry's mouth for hours faltered then faded completely. Her eyes dimmed to the depth of cloud-cast sea. Even hair matured to ripe gold by sun raying through glass on to a plaited halo was subdued into a dull glow when the earth seemed to move, taking all the joy from her wonderful day.

Was he asking *her* to offer herself as a piece of

marriageable merchandise? she wondered dully. Had he—the product of a race who regarded a marriage of convenience much more favourably than the union of a man with a woman whose only *dot* was a selfless, abiding love—decided that the call of duty could no longer be ignored, that he needed a meek, healthy wife and that she fitted the bill exactly?

'Why,' she whispered, wanting her suspicion confirmed, 'should a wealthy, eligible bachelor have to *buy* himself a wife?'

Ignoring the neighbouring family of diners, he reached across the table to capture her hands in his.

'Youth, sex, and beauty are too readily available,' he explained without a smile to soften the pain of his indifference. 'The qualities of loyalty, forbearance, and serenity are rare, and like all coveted objects must be bartered for and sold to the highest bidder.'

Cherry wished her limbs were not so leaden so that she might jump to her feet and run from the silver-tongued devil who adopted such a bewildering number of guises. Even wished that his proposition had been put forward yesterday when, like a sleepwalker, she had moved, talked, and suffered in his company, totally unaware that she had fallen in love with him . . .

'What you actually wish to acquire is a wife who will provide you with a shield of respectability and *carte blanche* to carry on living your life as you have always done,' she said huskily, painfully conscious of a lean brown finger monitoring the frenzied antics of a pulse hammering inside an encaged wrist. 'What inducement can you offer a wife in exchange?'

'A home, security for the rest of her life, children . . .!' He shrugged. 'What more can any woman ask?'

'A couple must make love to make children!' Cherry willed her eyes not to waver, but was glad that the table was hiding open weave sandals showing toes curled up tight with embarrassment. 'Surely the prerequisite for making love is to care . . .?'

'The betrothed of good is evil; the betrothed of life is death; the betrothed of love is divorce,' Lucien quoted dryly, displaying a hardbitten cynicism that caused her last faint hope to fade. 'Scientists have proved to their own satisfaction, and to mine, that the magical mystery of falling in love is in reality no more than the stimulating effect of extra light and warmth, especially in springtime, upon the output of hormones. As chemical changes sharpen the reproductive instinct, females are overwhelmed by an emotion they call love but which more matter-of-fact males regard merely as the mating instinct. If you compare the giddy passions of infatuation with the "high" experienced by drug addicts, and the crash that follows the end of an affair with drug withdrawal, you will be able to view the whole subject of love from a clinical aspect, just as I have learned to do.'

It seemed prophetic when, after they left the restaurant intending to make their way into the Jardin d'Acclimatation, the sun became enveloped by a bank of cloud that had been lurking on the horizon since early morning. They were lingering in the enclosure to allow Cherry to pet a brown cow mooing a plea to be fed when the first drops of rain splashed down on to her bare forearm.

'Here, take my jacket! If we hurry we might manage to find shelter before the heavens open.' Ignoring her protest, Lucien flung the jacket around her shoulders and anchored an arm around her waist to ensure that she kept pace with him when he began running towards a conglomeration of stalls, roundabouts and arcades set up to provide a wonderland of children's amusements.

His shirt was clinging to his body like a second skin when he swept her to a panting standstill beneath a huge striped awning fluttering gaily as a parasol over a display of toys, games and children's bric-à-brac. Lucien's attention was instantly attracted by the antics of an activated clockwork clown riding a bicycle, by preening cats, birds singing and swaying on their perches, and by an old-fashioned tin train chugging slowly and noisily around a circular track.

'I used to have toys such as these in my nursery,' he confided with a glint of boyish enthusiasm that made Cherry's heart somersault. He left her hugged within his coat to join an audience of excited children hanging over a waist-high barrier that had been erected just a short arm's length away from the mechanical performers, and as his dark storm-tossed head bent to exchange some remark with a small fellow enthusiast, she spied a look of absorption and pleasure animating his features.

A wave of weakness washed over her. She shuddered, trying to fight off the insanity of believing that the freedom-loving socialite could be capable of becoming a loving, indulgent father, a man who would treasure the company of children

whose presence would create for him the atmosphere of *bonne entente* that had been absent from
his life since the loss of the small animal that had
been his closest companion.

Nervously she stroked the sapphire-studded
wings of the butterfly ring that seemed to have
become a permanent part of her finger, seeking to
exploit its power as an antidote to the insane
temptation to grab and be grateful for the neglect,
indifference, and hurt which were the only rewards
she could expect from a clinically arranged
marriage.

Diana had been right to accuse her of
cowardice, to challenge her ability to gamble with
chance and risk the consequences, for in spite of a
craving for a home of her own, for children of her
own; in spite of her boast that she could live quite
happily with a man as ugly as a toad provided he
was prepared to offer her both, she was now faced
with the fact that the drum she had so confidently
beaten had been proved hollow . . .

'Come back to reality, sweet Charity! Are you
daydreaming about the ideal or pondering upon
the possible? Regretting, perhaps, that for most of
us life can only be extended, second-rate melodrama with a script calling for perpetual com-
promise.'

Charity returned to earth with a start, shocked
by his apparant ability to tune in to her
wavelength, and saw that he was standing, looking
gravely ridiculous, holding aloft a garish child's
umbrella.

'Take it,' he handed it to her with a grin.
'Dignity must be sacrificed to the need to keep
your golden tresses dry.'

Adapting as casually as she was able to his mood of frivolity, she responded with a dimpling smile:

'As you care so little about appearances, why don't *you* carry it for me?'

'As you wish,' he promptly agreed, then shattered her newly won composure when, with his mouth still smiling but with eyes that had regained some of their former gravity, he cautioned. 'Even today, in some parts of my country, this simple act is regarded as a preliminary of courtship. Any young man seeing a girl he fancies at a fair or religious festival can offer to carry her umbrella. If she accepts, he is allowed to buy her refreshments and to keep her company for the rest of the day. Provided her parents signify their approval by inviting him to stay for supper when he escorts the girl home that evening, he can consider himself betrothed. For a young man to carry a girl's umbrella as they walk together along a road is to advertise the fact that they are seriously contemplating marriage.'

Cherry found it hard to conceal her shyness of him during the following hours while they wandered in close proximity around the funfair; laughing together at the antics of dolphins in the zoo; lingering entranced by the performance of dancing marionettes; spending an enchanting half hour watching a simple play enacted by the cast of a children's theatre, then finally strolling hand in hand along paths in a delightful garden spread out within muted earshot of a sweetly melodious river.

It seemed a fitting climax to a day spent reviving childhood memories, a day to be ringed on her calendar as one of the happiest she had ever spent, when they rode on a toy train back to the edge of the Bois de Boulogne and then on to the Métro where they boarded a half empty train to be driven back to the city.

Feeling tired yet blissfully happy, Cherry smiled shyly at the man who had caused her emotions to become as mixed and unsettled as the weather.

'I shall never forget this wonderful day, Lucien. Thank you so much for pandering to my whim.'

'I too have had a pleasing time, *ma chérie*.' Her heart stirred at the sight of black tousled hair falling on to his brow, at the casually unbuttoned shirt and discarded jacket that lent him a youthful, carefree look that she had never previously associated with the cynical, world-weary Duc. 'In fact,' he sounded slightly surprised, 'I cannot remember ever having enjoyed an outing more. All that is needed to make this day truly memorable,' he leant closer to coax, 'is your admission that you are now ready to add the role of *duchesse* to your repertoire.'

Feeling bedevilled by eyes urging her to give in to temptation, she attempted to erect a last, swift barrier against insanity.

'I'm not sure what your proposition entails exactly . . .' she quivered doubtfully.

'Not proposition—proposal,' he corrected sternly. 'What I am asking, Charity Sweet, is: please, will you marry me?'

CHAPTER TEN

As the plane skimmed low over the deep blue
serenity of the Baie des Anges Cherry caught her
first glimpse of the small green island encircled by
woodland and fringed with sandy coves which, for
the unforeseeable future, was to be her home. Less
than a week had passed since Lucien had
persuaded her to accept his proposal, and just a
few tense hours ago, during a short, impersonal
civil ceremony, he had steadied her shaking hand
in order to slide a broad band of ownership upon
her finger.

Only Cécile and a male companion of Lucien's
whose name had not registered had been present to
witness an act she had been charmed into
committing in haste, but which during the past
few reflective hours she had begun bitterly
regretting.

Her thoughts were interrupted by the crackle of
static followed by Lucien's voice being relayed
from the cockpit to direct her attention below.

'If you look towards the northernmost tip of the
island you will see a spur of rock curving inward
forming a small natural harbour. From that point,
begin tracing a direct course east past the coastal
belt of trees, across central acres of farmland, and
there on the opposite coast you can just see the
roof of the château rising above trees clustered
around the grounds to protect the gardens from
the ravages of the *mistral*.'

Willing her quivering nerves to subside, Cherry peered downward in the direction he had indicated and experienced a leap of fear at the sight of forbidding stone walls etched against the skyline, a massive sweep of towers, turrets, and crenellated walls that gave an unmistakable impression of a fortress, the stronghold of a satyr—one of the lusty forest demons who were purported to have been the attendants of Bacchus.

The parallel her overwrought imagination had drawn between the freedom-loving Duc and the mythical god of pleasure seemed even more apt when the plane swooped low over a magnificent yacht anchored in solitary splendour inside the protective arm of rocks. She blinked, dazzled by glare bouncing off rippling water, pristine paint-work, polished metal handrails and glittering brass fittings.

'How does she strike you, *ma chérie*?' Lucien called out proudly. 'Soon I will introduce you to the pleasure of sailing, to the sort of freedom that can only be enjoyed beneath a wide sweep of sky that renders life timeless as each day appears to merge with the one before or the one following after. At no other time do I feel more vitally alive, more contented and well-disposed towards my fellow men. Never is my hunger better appeased than when I exist on a diet of freshly caught fish, sticks of bread, and a few carafes of rough red wine!'

Cherry could have responded simply by clicking a switch attached to a link-up microphone, but reaction to her folly had fastened a tight cold grip upon limbs that felt lifeless, reactions rendered numb. Vaguely, as the plane lost height and the ground rose up to meet them, she registered a scattering of cottages, each hemmed in by a walled garden and tucked between folds in the landscape out of sight of its neighbours; paths twisting in and out, disappearing around boulders, then emerging unexpectedly to cut bald swathes through blossoms casting a cloak of golden colour over cliffs inclining gradually upwards from the rocky shoreline.

Then a flash of vivid colour caught her eye and as the nose of the plane dipped towards a long swathe of green that was obviously a landing strip she was able to make out a car being driven at speed from the direction of the château by a girl dressed in one of the strong bright colours favoured by Mistral.

'Prepare to don your mantle of dignity for the very first time,' Lucien's voice confirmed her fears, 'Mistral appears eager to extend a welcome to the new *duchesse*.'

Mentally blessing Cécile and her staff for the speed with which they had provided her with the nucleus of a wardrobe of chic elegance designed to boost the confidence of its wearer, Cherry ran a nervous hand over the skirt of a cornflower blue suit and experienced the decadent thrill of feeling rich pure silk caressing her skin, clinging lovingly to breasts whose voluptuous contours had delighted Cécile and influenced Lucien in his search for a wife whose main function was to be a fruitful bearer of a line of healthy, attractive heirs.

'Ma belle Madone!' Cécile had christened her, obviously delighted by the elusive aura of innocence reflecting from a creation that had been designed for a virgin to wear at her wedding.

How sharply Lucien had frowned, Cherry mused, as the plane touched down and taxied to a slow, whining standstill, how swiftly he had leapt to the defence of a bride whose character he had apparently considered had been badly misjudged by the old lady whose powers of perception he had previously applauded.

'Innocence is all right in theory, Cécile,' he had snapped as he had slid a protective arm around his blushing bride before scaring the colour from her cheeks, by concluding, 'but experience has a lot going for it!'

Mistral had not been within call when Lucien had telephoned instructions to his staff to have the château prepared for the arrival of a new *duchesse*, so as she stepped down from the plane Cherry prepared herself to face the natural resentment of a relative whose acquaintance with the news had been second-hand. But the tortured squeal of brakes followed by the furious slamming of a door as Mistral erupted from the car gave fair indication that the intervening hours, far from helping to cool her temper, had fanned it into the sort of tempest after which she had been named.

'*Alors!*' Dark eyes spitting the fury of a tormented cat were trained upon Lucien as she rushed towards him, looking ready to rake scarlet fingernails across his faintly mocking features. 'Is it not enough to have made me the laughing stock of Riviera society by deliberately flaunting your affair with this . . . this . . . *chercheur d'or*,' she spat towards Cherry, 'without humiliating me further by bringing her here! Maman will be furious,' she choked, 'if ever she discovers that you have gone

so far as to install one of your *petites amies* under
the same roof as myself!'

Appalled as she was by Mistral's display of
naked jealousy and by the unpleasant experience
of hearing herself referred to as a gold-digger,
Cherry's understanding nature reacted with pity
towards the girl whose inability to control
emotions see-sawing between passionate maturity
and foolish adolescence had clamped a mask of
cold distaste upon Lucien's features.

'Do I have to remind you,' he condemned with
an edge as sharply honed as the dreaded guillotine,
'that the observations you have just made were
directed towards my wife, the Duchesse de
Marchiel, whose position entitles her to demand
that your impudent presence should be banned
immediately from the château that is now her
home?'

Either Lucien's previous spoiling was at fault, or
Mistral's wilful nature was immune to threats,
because she swiftly reacted by stamping her foot as
if to lay emphasis upon her scornful taunt.

'If you had intended society to take your new
duchesse seriously, you would not have publicised
quite so freely in the past your intention to settle
for maternal mediocrity in a wife and to continue
seeking excitement outside marriage. Everyone is
aware of and is amused by the knowledge that the
powers of the new Duchesse de Marchiel are as
provisional as those bestowed upon a novice
yacht-hand who, when sailing in French waters, is
lawfully entitled to take over from the owner
provided he or she is a member of his family or his
established concubine!'

Waves of humiliation swept over Cherry as,

ignored by the self-absorbed antagonists, she stood gasping, her secret barely acknowledged hopes of happiness dashed by the cruel disclosure that Lucien's intentions were known not only to his wife but also to the whole of French society.

A red rise of guilt was visible beneath Lucien's tan when he snarled back:

'Can a man no longer jest with friends without fear of being made to account to his wife for his bachelor humour?' he challenged, incensed, Cherry felt certain, by the first note of censure he had ever been called upon to endure.

'Not if his jokes are tantamount to a confession!' Mistral capped triumphantly. 'I suspect, Lucien, that your taste in humour is already imposing a great strain upon the affections of your wan-faced wife!'

This taunting reminder of his eavesdropping bride sent his angry eyes swivelling to examine a pale pinched face, a soft bottom lip gnawed by fretful teeth into a livid pink bruise, and wide blue eyes robbed of all sparkle by shocked incredulity.

'Get out of my sight, Mistral,' he ordered savagely, without shifting his glance from Cherry's face, *'or so help me, I'll . . .!'*

This time, Mistral was quick to heed the message of danger being transmitted from a strangled voice, from the thrust of a jaw that looked cast from iron. Lucien waited until her defiant figure had flounced out of sight, then strode towards the car she had abandoned to instruct tersely:

'Get in. Further comment can be saved for the privacy of the château.'

The short drive was accomplished in a matter of

minutes, too short a time to allow Cherry to
disperse the mist of tears that turned an imposing
frontage into a shimmering mirage. She winced
from the savagery of anger displayed by the
grating of gears and by the squeal of brakes
protesting against the slam of a foot that could
have dislodged an anchor, and shrank from the
bite of fingers into her forearm as she was bundled
up a flight of shallow stone steps and over an
imposing threshold.

'Marchez! Vite! Vite!' With explosive force
Lucien dispersed a retinue of servants lined up to
greet the new *duchesse* to the four corners of the
château, then releasing her arm, he strode across
the width of the hall towards high double doors
with heavily carved panels, obviously expecting
her to follow.

But she remained rooted, stunned by the impact
of surroundings so majestic she felt dwarfed, as
shrunken and scared as Alice who had swigged
from a bottle labelled: *Drink me!*

She had stepped through the main entrance of
the château directly into what appeared to be a
hall of honour, with the Marchiel family crest
displayed prominently over each door and portraits
of uniformed ancestors lining dark blue walls
towering so high she had to tip back her head to
follow their progress towards the spot where they
became scalloped by the drooping, gold-painted
arches of a domed ceiling.

Between each portrait were placed the crossed
swords, lances, cutlasses, and other items of
ancient weaponry that had probably been used by
the family of warriors whose painted features,
mottled by sunlight streaming through stained

glass windows, held for Cherry the familiarity of a
half-forgotten dream—until she recalled the grim,
flint-eyed, thin-lipped expression of determination
that clamped down heavily as a visor upon
Lucien's features whenever he began preparing his
rapier sharp tongue for combat.

Her bemused eyes wandered from the expanse
of black, veined marble floor to linger upon the
stained glass window, attempting to decipher the
legendary tales depicted in its colourful and
exquisitely executed panels. She had managed to
identify Poseidon and the Nereids emerging from
the sea when her attention was attracted by a
musical tinkle that drew her eyes aloft to stare
with startled admiration at an enormous golden
chandelier festooned with crystal baubles and
slender icicles that had been set into musical
motion by the draught from the open doorway.

'Cherry, would you come in here, please?' When
Lucien reappeared on the threshold of the room he
had previously entered he was scowling, looking as
imperious as the painted images of former Ducs de
Marchiel, who looked as if they would have fought
to the death in defence of family honour.

Feeling completely overawed, Cherry tiptoed
guiltily as an interloper across the hall of the ducal
palace to follow him inside a library with books
crammed into endless glass-fronted bookcases,
lined upon shelves reaching from the floor up to a
gallery giving access to further tightly packed
rows of richly bound volumes, many bearing the
coat of arms of the Marchiel hierarchy. A further
selection was piled upon a table topped with rich
brown leather encircled by a set of six matching
chairs, and one large tome was spread open on top

of a desk that looked so immovably huge she glanced downward, expecting to see roots striking from its ancient base.

But as Lucien was obviously in no mood to be amused she kept the fanciful notion to herself and stood with eyes downcast, feeling like a martyr unjustly condemned to be enveloped by a fire of flaming temper.

'I must apologise for Mistral's shocking behaviour,' he jerked, pacing the floor with the ranging stride of a beast thirsting for vengeance, 'the remarks she made are unforgivable!'

Fearful of the effect his anger might have upon Mistral's sensitive immaturity, and provoked by her own nervous tension, she blurted:

'I think you're being unfair. Mistral was upset and perhaps rather too outspoken, nevertheless, she spoke what she believed to be the truth. You told me yourself,' she reminded him gravely, 'that society, custom, and duty demand of every young, single Frenchman that he should take a wife. So surely, given such circumstances, speculation becomes unavoidable. You and I both know, Mistral and the whole of society must have guessed, that the only reason you married me was to provide an heir to your dukedom.' She hesitated, then drew in a deep breath before continuing bravely: 'Your rakish reputation has made you public property, Lucien. In the past you have flaunted convention, scoffed at adverse publicity, sought deliberately to shock by allowing your pet theories to be exaggerated in cold print— don't you think it's rather late to begin reacting to publicity like some indignant private individual?'

If a lamb had suddenly sprouted horns he could

not have been more startled. His prowling footsteps jolted to a standstill as he swung round to spear a look of incredulous hauteur at her.

'Are you suggesting that a bachelor drone who has lived all his life in a beehive, entering by the same door as hundreds of others, yet existing in a lonely cell, cannot expect to be afforded seclusion when he marries? I don't wish to turn my home into a fortress,' he snapped furiously, 'nor do I wish to live like my imprisoned ancestor who was condemned to wear a *masque de fer* even in the presence of the woman his jailors provided to make his banishment more bearable, but I refuse to allow my proud family name to be bandied about the market place, nor shall my wife be made the subject of snide comment or my marriage be viewed like a play staged specifically for the entertainment of a sensation-hungry audience! My next public appearance,' he declared, striding towards her, 'will be deliberately arranged to advertise the fact that I married not for reason or prudence, but solely from inclination!'

When his angry grip fastened upon her shoulders Cherry was jolted by the shock of discovering that her life had developed a very short fuse, that her hitherto serene and uncomplicated existence had become threatened by his explosive temper.

The grip of his fingers dug painfully into the tender flesh of her shoulders as he commanded thickly: 'The time has come when you must cease acting, *ma chérie*.' Roughly he pulled her towards him. 'It is time to draw the final curtain upon the unawakened child you portrayed for Henri, and upon the image of angelic innocence you somehow managed to implant in the mind of Cécile. I am in need of a wife who is all woman . . .!' She quivered in panic from the heat of his breath against her cheek, from eyes smouldering a message of purpose, of anticipated pleasure, of intimacy—and much more that it was beyond her ability to decipher. 'I want a child conceived in passionate consummation,' he threatened throatily, supporting her trembling, strength-sapped body against his lean hard trunk while he imprisoned with his lips a panicking butterfly pulse fluttering madly in her throat.

Torrid seconds later she was incapable of delving into his motives, had been rendered blind to reason, deaf to doubt, by an expert seducer whose kisses and caresses had introduced her into a limbo of bliss, a state of feverish upheaval in which her distracted senses could not cope with the true import of the message contained in his softly breathed promise:

'Tonight, *ma chérie*, when I introduce you to Riviera society, I'll wager you will no longer be able to fool them as you did Cécile into thinking that your lovely, ice-cool body has never melted in the heat of a man's desire!'

Her sensation of floating on a passion-dark cloud increased into a dizzying spiralling when he swept her off her feet, using his mouth to silence her weak moan of protest, to carry her out of the library, across the hall, and up a flight of stairs whose banisters formed part of a kaleidoscope of dark blue walls, frowning ancestral portraits, and a swirling white and gold ceiling.

Fear fought with longing, dread with trust, cowardice with courage, but when he strode with her inside a bedroom whose magnificence was dominated by a sculptored and gilded bed with gold brocade drapes looped from a high, impressive canopy she managed to choke out a protesting: 'No . . .!'

Gently, he lowered her to her feet but kept his arms around her waist, holding her prisoner until she was forced to meet his smouldering gaze.

'A wife cannot say "no" to her husband, *mignonne*,' he reminded softly. 'When a woman gives her consent in the marriage vows the law gives her husband a sexual right to her body for as long as their union lasts. *Bon gré, mal gré*— willingly or unwillingly, whether one will or will not!' The quoted motto held a faint ring of steel. 'You must forget the man whose treatment has left you emotionally repressed and remember that it is your duty to respond as actresses are taught to do, so that you exist in your act until your act becomes yourself, and there is no other you.'

She wanted to plead that she could not act and that even the mechanics of sex were unknown to her, but when Lucien's mouth descended warm and demanding upon hers, communicating desire and violently leashed passion, a sweet flame of wantonness shocked her dumb, an exquisite pain of warning that shot through her body just before a furnace of feeling erupted, coursing molten heat to the tip of every quivering nerve.

With accomplished ease he dealt with a zip, then with one vital button that loosened at his touch so that shimmering silk fell with a whispered protest to splash deep blue colour against a stretch of pale cream carpet. Cherry closed her eyes in an agony of shyness when her breasts were exposed to his

sensuous eyes, then reacted with voluptuous ardour
to the stroke of his firm hands against her thighs,
gasping a shock of sheer yearning as she lifted a
naked and tormented face to be kissed, offered her
body to be loved and caressed as a wife, to be taken
as a mistress, or simply to be used as an established
concubine had been used by the Duc whose true
feelings had remained hidden behind a mask of iron.

As she had discovered on the day he had taught
her how to swim, Lucien was an enthusiastic and
expert tutor. Tenderly, judging exactly the right
moment to advance her progress, he guided her
through each new stage of loving, teaching her the
rules of taking and of giving, showing patience
with her confusion, rewarding her progress with
kisses and low, shaken phrases, wiping her
emotional slate clean of established concepts so
that she began equating ecstasy with pain, tears
with pleasure, despair with her immature inability
to demonstrate clearly her feelings of joy,
fulfilment and overwhelming love.

After a while, with passion temporarily spent, he
allowed her to rest, cradling her within the tender
circle of his arms, kissing gold-tipped lashes where
they fluttered against flushed cheeks, playfully
fanning damp tendrils of hair with his warm
breath until they formed into tight, cherubic
ringlets on her brow.

She offered no resistance to his teasing, but lay
with her cheek resting against his teak tanned
chest, wishing she could remain as she was,
bemused, quivering and contented until morning.

'Tell me, *mignonne*, he murmured, his words
approaching her ears on soft cat's paws, 'when we
made love, were you playing a role, responding as an

actress to a stand-in for a star performer, or did you feel you were part of a love affair *d'un grand sérieux?*'

Fingers idling possessively amongst fine dark hairs spread across his chest fell suddenly still. If ever there was a right time to confess to duplicity surely it had to be now, when his mood was receptive, when contentment had left him purring, replete as a tiger lazily disinclined to growl.

But did she *want* to expose her shy inexperience to a man who had made no secret of his preference for women of the world, for sophisticates who played the mating game according to rules calling for pleasure on demand with no guilty reproaches, no proprietorial rights, no expectations of permanent commitment.

'*You are exactly the person I need to act out a role calling for quick wits, dedication and an ability to perform without blushing should circumstances ever warrant a bold display of hypocrisy*'.

His words echoed formally as the clause of a contract, reminding her that employment was all he had ever offered, convincing her that she dared not risk arousing either his displeasure or his embarrassment with an unwanted declaration of love.

Dropping a golden veil of lashes over eyes surging with regretful tears, she slid closer into the embrace of the man who had introduced her to her secret self, to a stranger who had lurked unseen, just as teeming, turbulent life seethes unnoticed beneath a surface of calm blue ocean, and managed to lie convincingly.

'A love affair *d'un grand sérieux*? Of course not, Lucien! Haven't you warned me often enough never to regard our alliance as anything more than *une passade . . .?*'

CHAPTER ELEVEN

As Cherry leant against the rail of a yacht ferrying herself and Lucien across the night-bewitched waters of the Mediterranean towards the fairytale principality of Monaco she was feeling nervous and bemused as a shopgirl who had somehow managed to become horribly miscast as the star of some Hollywood spectacular. How Diana would laugh if she could see her now, she thought, fingering—as if to convince herself that it was real and not just a figment of her imagination—a skirt of richly-rustling taffeta glowing golden as amber beneath the rays of a gloriously bright full moon. Part of a gown that even a queen would envy, a costly regal creation that was enveloping her trembling body in a widely swirling, sumptuously rustling armour of chic elegance. And how quick Diana would be to recognise and to sneer at the parallel between her present circumstances and the scenario that had been outlined by Marcus of the showgirl and the prince; the well-known star with a completely unknown and inexperienced girl as his leading lady.

'I must say, 'Lucien eyed her thoughtfully, 'you appear to possess the aptitude of a chameleon who changes its outlook according to prevailing surroundings. On the beach I've seen you romping like a child in shorts and a tee-shirt with a frivolous strawberry motif. This morning, you appeared like an apprehensive child-bride dressed in angelic blue. But Henri, had he been privileged to be present in our bedroom,' he puzzled gravely, 'would not have hesitated to award you one of his daring black lace garters. Yet at this moment, I feel I might run the risk of frostbite were I to attempt to penetrate your amber-bright shell of dignity.'

He could not have seen the blush that gave lie to this theory, yet showing no trace of his professed diffidence he turned from the rail to enfold her silken, perfumed elegance into an urgent, almost angry, embrace.

'What are you, *ma chérie*?' His puzzled eyes raked features silvered by moonbeams into a pale, calm mask. 'A deceiving witch, or merely an aggravating, immature bundle of contradictions?'

When his mouth lowered as if he was preparing to spend all evening finding out, Cherry found wits enough to eject a shaken whisper.

'Didn't you make certain before you offered me employment that I was a versatile actress, capable of enacting a variety of roles?'

His head jerked up, as if the reminder had jabbed sharply as a dagger into a conscience made complacent by a pupil's willingness to master every lesson set by her tutor. In spite of her fear of becoming a slave to his every whim, just another name to be written into the little black book every jet-setting socialite considered an essential aid to memory, she suffered a pang of regret when he released his grasp upon her waist and stepped sharply backward, allowing a yard of offended space to yawn between them.

'Thank you for the reminder,' he acknowledged

coldly, 'the very fact that it was necessary can be regarded as a sure indication that, when seeking out a perfectionist in pretence, I did my homework well. Your professionalism astounds me, *ma belle*,' he rasped harshly. 'Such dedication to one's art deserves to be rewarded with the sort of surprise that has been arranged to coincide with your first visit to Monaco!' With his features set into an expressionless mask he made plain his determination not to be drawn further by abruptly changing the subject.

'The fairyland of illuminated shops, arcades, and floodlit orifices that you can see ahead, perched high upon a rock rising up out of the sea, is a realm of unreality, a miniature wonderland immensely rich in fantasy, a paradise of ancient narrow streets, gardens filled with perfume and flowers that know no seasons. A "once upon a time" place that has a prince living in a wedding-cake castle guarded by a tiny army of soldiers. A contradictory country that resounds in turn with the music of the world's finest orchestras, the noisy roar of the Grand Prix motor rally, the swell of operatic arias and the click of counters and the tinkling of tokens being disgorged from the Casino's slot machines.'

'I've read about the fabulous parties that are held at the Sporting Club,' Cherry schooled her tone to match his tone of bored familiarity, but did not succeed in eliminating a thrill of excited anticipation, 'and about the cabarets that are held in the Casino and the Café de Paris. Will we have time to visit them, do you think?'

'Where else?' His stern mouth softened, disarmed by her air of suppressed excitement. 'Tonight I am introducing my new wife to Riviera society. We will be appearing briefly at each of the rendezvous where socialites gather, staying just long enough to arouse their curiosity, allowing them to glimpse, but not to speak to or touch, killing off malicious speculation with a display of affection and deep engrossment, so that no one will ever again question whether our marriage was anything other than a love match.'

Cherry willed herself not to sway towards him when he rejoined her at the ship's rail where, with arms almost touching, they watched the jewelled fantasy world of Monaco rearing larger by the minute as the skipper headed the yacht towards harbour. She waited, wanting to move away yet held in the grip of physical languor.

Lucien, too, seemed to be having difficulty controlling an impulse to touch her whenever the slightest excuse made contact permissible—allowing their hands to brush in passing; dusting an imaginary speck from her shoulder; twisting a wisp of soft golden hair around his finger under the pretext of sweeping it back from her brow. The tension between them was raw, stretched taut as elastic which, if ever it should snap, would catapult them into swift, close unity.

She remained still, hardly daring to breathe as the force of his magnetism jumped like a sparking live wire towards her, seeking a collision or even the most delicate of contacts, which would blow a fuse on their carefully controlled emotions.

'Mignonne . . .!'

Every pulse in her body leapt in response to a hesitancy in his voice that was totally un-characteristic. But whatever he had intended to say was drowned by the blaring of a ship's hooter as the yacht began nosing inside a crowded harbour. Cherry saw him shrug with annoyance, then reached out to lift something from a chair set in a shadow-shrouded corner of the deck.

'Here, put this on.'

She felt the brush of fur against her neck and the weight of a coat settling around her shoulders.

'The night breeze can grow chilly,' he continued, 'and there is no place for a woollen shawl in your elegant ensemble.'

In spite of his jesting words his dark eyes were sombre when she jerked round to face him with a gasp of surprise. Without having to look, she had recognised the feel of the silken sable pelts she had paraded in once before for the benefit of the *paparazzi*.

'But, Lucien, I can't wear this, it's far too ... too ...'

'Erotic?' he suggested whimsically. 'But eroticism is what the world expects of the wife of a wealthy man. It is the reason crowds gather around the fringes of high society, to stare and envy possessions they know they can never hope to own themselves. You must get used to the idea of becoming part of a peepshow, *ma petite*,' he rebuked with a touch of irony, 'one of a circus whose performers are expected to appear spectacularly dressed before an astute and fiercely critical audience.'

Cherry shuddered from the stroke of glossy brown sable that made her feel possessed, a piece of property belonging to the rich and famous Duc de Marchiel. Suddenly, the gifts he had lavished upon her assumed a new perspective—the amber gold dress whose rich formal elegance had pleased him so much; the suite of sapphire jewellery that he had insisted she should wear; the sensational Russian sable costing more than she could have earned working six years non-stop, had not been intended to give pleasure but were mere items of window-dressing, a planned pretext to a parade of costly possessions.

'Brace yourself, *ma chérie*,' he murmured as the yacht began nosing into what appeared to be the only berth left vacant in a crowded harbour, 'news of our arrival has attracted the usual unsavoury reception committee!'

Even as she followed his gaze down to a crowded quayside lights began exploding in her face, the harsh blue glare of flashbulbs popping from cameras held by a score of photographers jostling and gesticulating as they fought to obtain the best camera angle. A surprised breath rasped in her throat as she realised for the very first time the invasion of privacy, the lack of anonymity that had to be endured by people in order to satisfy the appetite of magazine readers such as herself whose interest in the affairs of members of high society was insatiable.

'Let's give them something really torrid to splash across their front pages,' Lucien muttered, sounding as if his sorely tried patience had been stretched to breaking point. Fiercely, he pulled her shocked, perfumed, sable-clad body into his arms. A solitary bulb flashed just as his dark head lowered towards her, illuminating a chiselled profile, determined mouth, and eyes demanding complete and unrestrained co-operation. But when his mouth fastened upon hers all thought of resistance was lost in a minefield of flashes and furore that exploded the moment their lips touched, a barrage of noise and emotional upheaval during which Lucien vented his built-up frustration in fierce kisses that drained her dry of strength and which, when he lifted his head, left her floundering in a vortex of vitally aroused desire.

'You respond promptly to your cue, as very good actresses should,' he sneered, expelling a long shaken breath while he held her swaying body erect. 'Making love to you starts me warring with my conscience. Afterwards I feel bad, plagued by a feeling that I am guilty of something immoral.'

Cherry experienced a foretaste of what the future held in store when, as soon as they stepped ashore, she and Lucien were surrounded by photographers and reporters firing questions so rapidly she had no time to formulate an answer.

'What does it feel like to be the new Duchesse de Marchiel?'

'How long have you been married?'

'Where were you married?'

'Do you intend starting a family right away?'

'What nationality are you, Madame la Duchesse, and what was your surname before you married?'

Expertly, Lucien forged a way through the crowd, looking determinedly goodhumoured, guiding Cherry within the circle of a protective arm until they reached a chauffeur-driven limousine waiting just a few yards away from where the yacht was berthed. For the first time in her life Cherry felt fear of fellow human beings as she was pushed and squeezed by an ever-tightening circle of reporters determined to obtain a scoop, to elicit just a few stammered words from the beautiful, ravishingly dressed, but obviously terrified young *duchesse*.

'Give us a break, *monsieur*!' one reporter wailed when finally they gained the security of the car. 'You owe it to your public!'

Nodding instructions to the chauffeur to drive off, Lucien wound down a window to deliver a polite parting shot.

'Not today, gentleman. My wife is unused to publicity. Perhaps in a week or so, when she has become accustomed to the pressure applied by pressmen, she may decide that she is ready to grant interviews.'

'*Never . . .!*'

As the car slid into soundless motion Cherry shook her head so vigorously that her sapphire butterfly earrings appeared in danger of soaring into flight.

'I never want to face such a terrifying mob again! Who are they, and how on earth did they know exactly where and when to meet us?'

'They are the infamous *paparazzi*, who pay servants to listen at keyholes and deckhands to report whenever a yacht is being prepared to leave port.' He leant back against cream leather upholstery to cast a look of puzzlement over her flushed and slightly dishevelled appearance.

'I had imagined you capable of showing more aplomb when coping with such a situation. After all,' her guilty conscience detected a challenge in his question, 'aren't actresses accustomed to the attentions of pressmen? Even those whose careers fall short of stardom must surely be familiar with the sort of treatment imposed by the press upon their peers? Yet you reacted to their presence like a startled rabbit, *ma chérie*.'

Suddenly the car seemed filled with his looming presence as he leant forward, blinding her vision with stern, dark features; a shoulder width of white dinner jacket; a black, impeccably knotted tie, and ice-blue glints radiating from one diamond-studded cufflink.

'Some women can lie so well they make the truth sound false. Nevertheless, I feel it is safe to assume that you would never lie to me, *petite*,' he assured her with a hint of threat that caused her bottom lip to quiver, 'especially when I tell you that of all human failings I consider deceit to be by far the least forgivable!'

With fingers trembling so much she could barely hold her compact steady, Cherry attempted to repair the damage done to her appearance. For some reason Lucien had become suspicious, of that she felt certain. The threat of reprisal contained in his words had filled her with dread, dread of the anger that would be sure to erupt if ever he were to find out about the lie of omission that had led him to conclude that she was an actress, skilled in the portrayal of pretence; that Ryan was her stepfather and not, as she had allowed him to believe, an unfaithful lover, but most of all dread of being banished from his life, especially now when she had only just realised the extent of her love for him.

By the time the car had begun sweeping in an arc around a lawn laid out with artistic, colourful flowerbeds and fringed with stately palms, she had managed to control tremors of apprehension that had left her body feeling thrashed. But when it drew to a standstill outside the main entrance to the Casino, nervousness returned in force at the sight of its magnificent floodlit façade adorned with statues, stretches of stone-sculptured balcony, and two ornate cupolas each bearing the colourful flag of Monaco towering either side of a huge clock with a stone-carved surround incorporating plinths providing a permanent resting place for two winged spirits.

Cherry needed the small amount of confidence afforded by the knowledge that her gown—created especially by Cécile for just an occasion—possessed a look of regality that demanded poised, composed grace from its wearer; that the precious deep blue butterflies swarming around her wrist and slender neck, nestling against each earlobe and upon one pale slender finger composed too costly a gift for any man, however wealthy to bestow upon a "passing fancy". And even Lucien had been moved to compliment her upon the elegance of a coiffure that had taken hours of shampooing, rinsing, drying and brushing before spun gold strands had been smoothed back severely from her face, twisted into plaits, then wound into a glistening coronet positioned high upon the crown of delicately contoured head.

She blinked and stumbled slightly when, as Lucien was assisting her out of the car, a battery of flashbulbs exploded around them.

'Stay calm,' Lucien murmured, as he stooped to scoop the train of her dress clear of the car, 'try to hang on to the air of cool serenity that makes me so proud to introduce you as my wife.'

Immediately, the faces of a jostling crowd of onlookers began appearing less hostile, their loud exclamations more friendly; the reporters and photographers becoming transformed from belligerent fiends into human beings bound by contracts of employment to produce results before receiving pay.

The smile that transformed her tense features into a slowly unfolding blossom of beauty was intended solely for Lucien, but was seized upon by a horde of enthusiastic men who stuck cameras in front of her face and pleaded:

'Hold that smile just a little longer, duchess!'

'Turn this way! Please, Madame la Duchesse, will you turn *this* way!'

'Great! May we have just one more shot of you smiling up at your husband?'

Her smiles had graduated into giggles of genuine amusement by the time she and Lucien had managed to outstrip the *paparazzi* who pursued them as far as the entrance to the casino. Hand in hand, and laughing with triumph, they erupted into a huge salon filled with people milling around great Ionic columns supporting a gallery decorated with bronze vases spilling with blazing crystal candelabra. Her smile faded as she gazed upward in awestricken silence at panelled doors lining both sides of the gallery, at pictures depicting olive pickers and fisherman and a beautiful grotto bathed in the subdued tones of twilight.

'This is the Atrium,' Lucien explained, his voice made matter-of-fact by long association. 'From here, we can take a lift to the Private Room where, I hope, the surprise I promised you will already be waiting.'

The Private Room! The very name was evocative of the sort of privilege demanded as a right by members of the exclusive social circle of aristocrats and dignitaries in which Lucien was a prime mover.

Cherry tried hard not to show how terrified she was by her lavish surroundings, how she had been made to feel inadequate and ill-at-ease by the unashamed curiosity of stares being directed from an assembly whose innate good breeding had been overwhelmed by an urge to monitor the shy but graceful progress of the new *duchesse*. Erecting a barrier of polite aloofness between himself and less courteous spirits who darted in their path, apparently determined to effect an introduction, Lucien acknowledged the greetings of a multitude of acquaintances who were not allowed to interrupt, much less halt, their approach towards a Belle Epoque lift which, Cherry registered fretfully, had probably been utilised by all the crowned heads of Europe since its inception during the beautiful era of the late nineteenth century.

When the doors closed behind them, allowing a few soaring seconds of privacy, Lucien tipped up her chin with one finger to gaze deeply into eyes dark as sapphire seas. and as teeming with uncertainty.

'You took your first hurdle well, *ma petite*,' he assured her gravely. 'Courage, like love, needs constant feeding, so you may gain confidence from the knowledge that your *ravissante* appearance has dislodged a sated society from its rut of tedium.'

Like a starving child tasting a first sip of honey, Cherry hungrily begged for more.

'Are you really satisfied with my performance, Lucien?' She blushed painfully when the hiss of his indrawn breath told her that he had read into her words a *double entendre*. Nevertheless she stumbled bravely on. 'I mean . . . are you satisfied in *every* way?'

Immediately the words were spoken she regretted giving in to a craving to hear him voice one brief word of love, to detect the slightest indication that, unlike his masked ancestor who had been *provided* with a female companion, he felt some emotional affinity with the woman destined to bear his child. But the only satisfaction to be gained from her ordeal was the convulsive tightening of fingers resting on her waist, before the lift doors opened upon a room lined with dark wooden panelling, its severity softened by strategically placed mirrors reflecting the glow of wall lights and low-slung candelabra; a pale gold ceiling, and fringed velvet drapes that picked up the subdued brown and gold tones of a carpet flowing beneath tables laid with tablecloths and place settings for a restricted number of diners.

One vivid splash of magenta jarred with the room's restful ambience. The colour of a dress being worn by a girl who rose to her feet when the lift doors opened and began sauntering with her male companion in their direction.

Mutual recognition was slow but ultimately startling.

'*Diana*! *Marcus*!' Exclaiming with pleasure, Cherry rushed to greet them.

'It can't be . . . *Cherry*?' When Diana jolted to a standstill Cherry had to laugh at her expression of stunned amazement.

'Of course it's me!' she affirmed with a gurgle. 'Oh, how pleased I am to see you looking so well, Diana. Obviously I've been worrying needlessly, your visit to the States appears to have done you good!'

'The same must apply to your extended stay in France.' In spite of her theatrical training Diana's smile appeared forced, her words wooden. 'You've changed out of all recognition, what on earth have you been up to while I've been away?'

Cherry's smile faltered as she recognised chagrin and undisguised envy in the way Diana's eyes glittered over the fabulous set of sapphires and a gown whose design and finish labelled it 'haute couture'.

Unconsciously appealing, she turned to Lucien, who responded by taking over control.

'Are you pleased with the surprise I planned for you, *ma chérie*?' Diana's mouth tightened when Lucien's arm tightened possessively around Cherry's shoulders. 'Marcus cabled me to arrange a meeting. Seemingly, his new production has been plagued with some difficulty which he appears to think can only be resolved by personal discussion.'

'Only because the conditions you had written into our contract before agreeing to become the majority backer made it impossible for me to act without your permission.' Marcus's harsh tone introduced a second note of discord into what should have been a happy reunion.

Cherry shivered, experiencing a chill of foreboding that seemed justified when Marcus coldly accused Diana:

'Had I been free to use my own discretion, I would not have hesitated to tear up the contract of a leading lady who discovered that the pleasures to be found amongst the lotus-eaters of Hollywood were infinitely preferable to the early morning calls

and strict adherence to time schedules demanded
by Hollywood film producers!'

'Even the insecurity of working in English rep is
preferable to living the sort of nun-like existence
you tried to impose upon me!' Diana flashed back.
'I've had Hollywood right up to here!' She sliced a
hand across her brow, then turned a contemptuous
shoulder upon Marcus.

'Cherry,' she instructed imperiously, 'as there's
no longer any need for you to be held hostage, I'll
wait until you've collected your belongings, then
we'll leave together on the first flight home!'

'Oh, but . . .' Cherry gasped into silence,
floundering in her search for the kindest possible
way to tell Diana that such a solution was no
longer possible.

Lucien, however, did not seem disposed to be
kind.

'Obviously, the affairs of French socialites are
not as widely reported in the States as they are in
Europe,' he iced, 'or you would by now have read
in the newspapers that the *hostage* you referred to
has voluntarily relinquished her freedom by
marrying me. Cherry will remain here with me, to
live for the rest of her life in the château that for
centuries has been the ancestral home of the Duc's
de Marchiel.'

It was just as well, Cherry concluded wryly, that
Diana's green-eyed stare of incredulity spoke for
itself, for shock appeared to have deprived her of
all power of speech. She had few illusions left
about her friend's true nature, nevertheless she was
unprepared for her spiteful, almost vicious reaction
to the startling news.

'You sly cat!' she accused Cherry. 'I never

dreamt you meant every word when you swore
you would be prepared to marry a man as ugly as
a toad provided he could offer you a home'. '*My
one ambition in life*,' she mimicked spitefully,
deliberately creating an impression that she was
quoting Cherry verbatim, '*is to have my own home,
my own children, and a provider who will be content
to remain in the background of my life*'.

'And what a provider!' Diana scoffed, tossing
Lucien a look of derision that cast a thunderous
cloud over features set inflexible as a mask and
twice as unreadable. 'Even a scheming opportunist
deserves to be congratulated upon the success of a
campaign planned to elevate her from the lowly
status of perfume seller in a department store to
the prestigious position of wife to the owner of—
amongst other things—one of the largest of the
perfume distilleries that has made the nearby town
of Grasse famed throughout the world as the
capital of the French perfume industry!

'Poor Lucien!' Her false pitch of laughter rasped
roughly as a file over Cherry's shocked nerves.
'How society will pity you when the news gets into
print that you've been double-crossed—as a snake
charmer is pitied when he's bitten by a snake!'

CHAPTER TWELVE

LUCIEN was furious. As they were being driven back to the yacht Cherry sat huddled in the back seat of the car, trying to make as much space as possible between herself and the husband whose features appeared clamped with the sort of iron-clad frigidity that had been imposed upon the ancestor who had been exiled for life on a tiny island, with a female companion who was not of his own choosing.

She curled her fists into tight balls, hoping the pain inflicted by pointed fingernails on the soft flesh of her palms might override the memory of a scene enacted within seconds—played by a leading lady who had managed to inject total conviction into a dialogue of false charges and half-truths—yet forcing repercussions that seemed fated to endure for a lifetime. Diana's worst act of treachery by far had been her implied threat of scandal, the emphasis she had placed upon certain words that had left her listeners in no doubt that, unless she was favourably rewarded, she would not hesitate to supply waiting press-men with a story that would be bound to make Lucien appear a fool, the laughing stock of Riviera society.

Yet, strangely, it had not been until Cherry had begun pleading with Diana that Lucien had become really angry, angry enough to bundle her into the lift, hurry her through a crowd of gaping onlookers, then out of the main door of the Casino where a score of re-galvanised pressmen had been dispersed with a savagely-bitten imprecation she had been too upset to interpret.

When they began driving along the quayside Cherry saw the ghostly bulk of the yacht looming out of the darkness. Immediately the car drew to a standstill she scrambled out and, with billowing skirts bunched between her fists, scurried up the gangplank and down an alleyway towards the stateroom in which—because their outing had been planned to extend into the early hours—they had arranged to spend the night.

Imagining the sound of Lucien's footsteps following closely behind her, she flung inside the stately appartment, banged the door shut and turned the key. With her back pressed against its panels she waited with bated breath for some evidence of his approach, but for long-drawn-out minutes the only sounds she could hear, other than the terrified thumping of her heart, were the throbbing of newly-fired engines, the clanking of an anchor chain, and a crewman's shouted instruction to cast off.

She sagged with relief, welcoming the respite afforded by Lucien's obvious decision to return at once to the island, then in an agony of misery ran sobbing towards the bed, collapsing face downward to weep until her aching heart felt drained and a pool of spent misery had spread a dark, damp stain across the silk of a pale blue coverlet.

She lost all track of time as she lay quiet, her body racked with dry sobs, and was almost too numb to notice when the vibrations of the engines suddenly ceased. But the unmistakable sounds of a tender, used to ferry passengers from the yacht across the shallow inshore waters around the island, being lowered into the water levered her upright. She sat poised, listening intently for some clue that might explain her sense of unease, a suspicion that the activity taking place above deck was the forerunner of something out of the ordinary. Then at the sound of a shouted farewell she ran to peer out of the porthole and was just in time to see the small boat carrying the skipper and the only two deckhands who had not gone ashore when the yacht had berthed disappearing towards the jewel-bright bulk of Monaco still glittering close by, just beyond a dark stretch of harbour.

She had no time to gather her wits before Lucien's firm footsteps preceded his sharp demand for entry.

'Would you kindly open the door and save me the trouble of having to look for a passkey?'

Feeling trapped, Cherry moved reluctantly to turn the key with a click that resounded in her ears like a pistol shot, then nervously backed away from the black-browed, tight-lipped figure that strode across the threshold.

'Why are you so determined to avoid a showdown?' Lucien challenged grimly. 'Is it because you are uneasy in the presence of truth and honesty, because you are happier hiding your shortcomings behind a veil of pretence?'

She clenched her teeth to prevent them from chattering. The moment of confrontation that had been hanging like the sword of Damocles over her head had at last descended. Yet in spite of her fear of his displeasure she felt an emotion akin to relief when she forced herself to take up his challenge.

'I did not lie. I've never lied to you, Lucien! You based your judgment of my character solely upon the time and place I chose to take a holiday, and upon an assumption that I shared the same talents and ambitions as Diana. Never once have you bothered to enquire about my views, about my own personal hopes, fears, likes or dislikes,' she gulped, feeling a second onrush of tears. 'Always you've treated me like a lump of unfeeling clay to be manipulated and moulded into whichever object—hostage, employee, actress, wife—you've happened to require at any given moment!'

She trembled into silence, bracing herself for tongue-lashing accusations of duplicity and deceit, for raging resentment of having been made to look a fool, for threats of reprisal for anything other than the spasm of feeling that dislodged his mask of cold disdain, revealing an emotion akin to pain, for his weary sigh, and hesitant, quietly voiced apology.

'I'm sorry you've found me such an insensitive brute, *ma chérie*.' She almost cried out in protest against the dispirited shrug of shoulders which even when flexing teak-tanned and bare had always maintained an unmistakable set of authority. 'For some time now I have been plagued with doubt, tormented by a suspicion that, although I have been allowed the privilege of enjoying your companionship, friendship, even your delightfully willing responses as a wife, you are destined to remain an enigma, an elusive will-o'-the-wisp who drifts within my reach but persistently evades capture. Is it fear or mistrust that forces you to keep me at arm's length?' he grated, leaping from gravity to resentment with the swiftness of a muscle jerking in his jaw, 'or is it the ghost of the faithless lover you call Ryan that urges you to retreat from total commitment? There is no easy passage to Utopia,' he reminded her grimly. 'Even sweet-smelling incense lies dormant until the scorch of flame releases its fragrance.'

A flicker of life stirred amongst the charred ashes of her hopes. Cherry did not stir, not even a breath disturbed her pale marble-stillness as she stared across the chasm of doubt dividing her and the jet-setting socialite whose name had become synonymous with lighthearted flirtation, fickle fancy, and dedicated resistance to matrimonial ties. It seemed barely believable that Lucien might actually be verging upon an admission of . . . *love*!

In a faint, shaken whisper she dared to test out her outrageous theory.

'I'd never been in love until I met you,' she admitted painfully. 'Ryan is the name of my stepfather.'

'*Diable*!' She jerked back in panic from his mutter of outraged aggravation, then, in spite of dark eyes sparking signals of danger, a lean body straining against leashed-in fury, she found the courage to stumble forward into the desperate embrace of arms that closed like a trap, crushing her close until her body seemed to melt into his— heart to heart, pulse to pulse, soft flesh merging into a taut masculine frame with muscles flexed, sinews tightening, and nerves pounding a message of urgent physical need.

'*Heartless, tantalising witch*!' he groaned against the soft, quivering mouth she offered up to be punished. 'How dared you prolong the torment imposed by thoughts of you pining for the love of some other man? *Women have been whipped for less!*'

He extracted his revenge with kisses that scourged, with slow sensuous caresses that stretched her endurance to the edge of torment, with husked endearments that flayed her senses, and with hungry, fire-flecked glances that stroked across passion-punished eyes, a crushed mouth, and stripped her young, vulnerable body bare of timidity. His chastisement was so deliberate and so thorough she had begun wilting beneath a weight of longing before he finally relented by swinging her high into his arms and lowering her gently on to the bed.

'I am far from ready to forgive you yet, *mon petit trésor*,' he scolded shakily. 'Complete absolution must wait until you have supplied proof that you love me just a fraction as much as I love you.'

'Darling Lucien!' Cherry teased with a wondering catch in her voice, 'a sceptic is rarely prepared to be convinced by verbal assurances, but prefers to eliminate all doubt by keeping in close and constant contact with his subject.'

Her blatant invitation did not go ignored by the deft-fingered man who sought for and undid a hidden waist-length zip so that stiff amber taffeta fell open like a shell disclosing a tender, pearl-pale secretion of treasure.

'*Je me consume pour toi, mon trésor!*' he hissed softly. 'We have talked enough—wasted far too much time!'

Blissful hours later, as she was lying curled close as a contented kitten listening to his steadily drumming heartbeat, Lucien stirred from his state of supreme satisfaction to stretch sideways, groping for some object just out of reach in the drawer of a bedside unit.

Cherry sighed, resenting the withdrawal of his animal warmth, then shivered with delight when his lips sought the smooth, sensitive curve of her shoulder.

'I have a wedding present for you, *mignonne*. I think this could be exactly the right moment for you to receive it.'

'A wedding present? But you've already given me so much!'

He smiled, lazily amused by a wife who was still able to blush as easily as a bride. 'But only one gift of any consequence, *mon ange*,' he assured her gravely, placing a small beribboned package in her hand. 'Many months ago the *célèbres parfumeurs* employed by Les Parfums de Marchiel created a masterpiece of perfume with a fragrance evocative of purity and passion, spice and sweetness—a blend of indefinable mystique which everyone agreed should not be marketed until an appropriate name could be found.'

Rendered slightly subdued by the seriousness of his tone, Cherry undid a bow of pale blue ribbon and carefully withdrew a small box from its nest of wrapping paper.

'Go on, open it!' Fighting distraction caused by the feathering of his lips across the tender nape of her neck, she lifted up the lid and stared, realising immediately the import of the gift and its timely presentation. With tear-bright eyes she examined a small sample bottle of perfume—liquid gold trapped within a heart of crystal—that had a label bearing a name stamped in a printed copy of Lucien's distinctive scrawl: '*Ma Chérie*'.

Lifting brimming eyes to meet his watchful gaze, she husked, unconsciously pleading: 'You must have decided some time ago to allow the perfume to share my name. *How* long ago, Lucien?' She waited tense as a bowstring, still too shy of him to put her hope into words.

'How long have I known that I was in love with you?' He pretended to take time to consider. 'I can't pinpoint the exact moment, but certainly it happened during the first day of your arrival in Cannes.' His simple statement shocked her dumb. 'Falling immediately and deeply in love was an unpleasant experience for me. For the first time in my life I found myself exhibiting all the symptoms of a lovesick calf, wanting to rush you off your feet yet forced to practise patience; following in your footsteps everywhere you went, watching, waiting, forced to bide my time because of the panic that erupted each time I manoeuvred myself near enough to gaze into your shy, beautiful eyes. In desperation, as the day of your departure loomed nearer, I resorted to ruthlessness by exploiting the needs of Marcus and Diana, by enlisting the aid of the unsuspecting *paparazzi*— even taking advantage of Mistral's youthful infatuation in a bid to prevent you from disappearing out of my life for ever,' he admitted without the slightest trace of shame.

'Yet you dared to accuse *me* of being deceitful! Dimly, Cherry began fathoming the extent of the ruthless determination that had earned his family the right to incorporate within their crest the arrogant motto: *Bon gré, mal gré*—willingly or unwillingly. Whether one will or will not! 'Does that mean that you've known all along that I'm not an actress?'

'*You*, an actress!' As he pulled her back into his arms she heard his deep throated growl of laughter. 'A professional actress can demonstrate joy and sorrow, hatred and love, even turn on tears to order, but one would need to be totally lacking in artifice and guile in order to copy your own adorably spontaneous blushes, *ma petite*.'

His arms tightened possessively around her unresisting body as he bent close to whisper a shaken promise:

'We've walked together through a wilderness of doubt, but now our journey is over, *ma chérie*. At last we have come home, home to where our new-found love will be strengthened and renewed with each rising of the sun over the ageless, ever-blue Baie des Anges!'

A WORD ABOUT THE AUTHOR

Margaret Rome's first Harlequin was published in 1969. Appropriately, it was entitled *A Chance to Win* (Harlequin Romance #1307).

But her chance was a while in coming. In her teens Margaret dealt with a long-term bout of rheumatic fever; then followed a series of manual jobs that "just could not satisfy my active mind," and finally marriage and the birth of a son. But at last, when Margaret did get down to the business of writing—beginning by doodling with pen and paper—she discovered that a sentence formed, a second one followed, and before long, paragraphs had developed into a chapter. "I had begun the first of many journeys," she says.

Today Margaret and her husband make their home in Northern England. For recreation they enjoy an occasional night out dancing, and on weekends they drive into the beautiful Lake District and embark on long, invigorating walks.

HARLEQUIN CLASSIC LIBRARY

Great old romance classics from our early publishing lists.

FREE BONUS BOOK

On the following page is a coupon with which you may order any or all of these titles. If you order all nine, you will receive a FREE book—*District Nurse,* a heartwarming classic romance by Lucy Agnes Hancock.

The fourteenth set of nine novels in the

HARLEQUIN CLASSIC LIBRARY

Great old favorites...
Harlequin Classic Library

Complete and mail this coupon today!

Harlequin Reader Service

In U.S.A.
1440 South Priest Drive
Tempe, AZ 85281

In Canada
649 Ontario Street
Stratford, Ontario N5A 6W2

Please send me the following novels from the Harlequin Classic Library. I am enclosing my check or money order for $1.50 for each novel ordered, plus 75¢ to cover postage and handling. If I order all nine titles at one time, I will receive a FREE book, *District Nurse*, by Lucy Agnes Hancock.

☐ 118   ☐ 121   ☐ 124
☐ 119   ☐ 122   ☐ 125
☐ 120   ☐ 123   ☐ 126

Number of novels checked @ $1.50 each =	$_____
N.Y. and Ariz. residents add appropriate sales tax	$_____
Postage and handling	$_____ .75
TOTAL	$_____

I enclose _____
(Please send check or money order. We cannot be responsible for cash sent through the mail.)
Prices subject to change without notice.

Name _____
(Please Print)

Address _____
(Apt. no.)

City _____

State/Prov. _____

Zip/Postal Code _____

Offer expires May 31, 1984   31156000000

BOOK MATE PLUS®

The perfect companion for all larger books! Use it to hold open cookbooks... or while reading in bed or tub. Books stay open flat, or prop upright on an easellike base... pages turn without removing see-through strap. And pockets for notes and pads let it double as a handy portfolio!

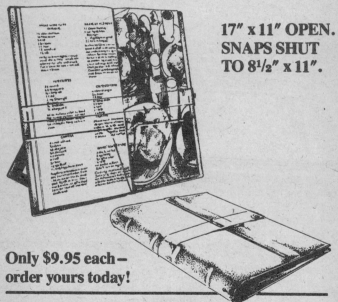

17" x 11" OPEN. SNAPS SHUT TO 8½" x 11".

Only $9.95 each— order yours today!

Available now. Send your name, address, and zip or postal code, along with a check or money order for just $9.95, plus 75¢ for postage and handling, for a total of $10.70 (New York & Arizona residents add appropriate sales tax) payable to Harlequin Reader Service to:

Harlequin Reader Service

In U.S.
P.O. Box 52040
Phoenix, AZ 85072-9988

In Canada
649 Ontario Street
Stratford, Ont. N5A 6W2